CW00421153

First edition June 2022

ISBN 9798449761552 (paperback)

So this is Love?

Maddie Richardson

Love as defined by the Oxford dictionary:

Senses relating to affection and attachment.

A feeling or disposition of deep affection or fondness for someone, typically arising from a recognition of attractive qualities, from natural affinity, or from sympathy and manifesting itself in concern for the other's welfare and pleasure in his or her presence (distinguished from sexual love at sense); great liking, strong emotional attachment; (similarly) a feeling or disposition of benevolent attachment experienced towards a group or category of people, and (by extension) towards one's country or another impersonal object of affection. With of, for, to, towards.

How far would you go for love?

Prologue

There was a scream.

A mother's scream as she watched the black car slam into the small body of her son. His face showed confusion and shock as he was lifted off the road and high into the air. The car slammed on its breaks, skidded to the left and juddered violently as it crumpled, passenger side first, into the back end of a school minibus. A deafening bang mingled with the sound of metal on metal as the airbags were deployed, the occupants stilled as the carcass of the car came to a final silent halt.

Time stood still.

Everything stopped except for the body of the boy as it fell from the sky, and landed on the road behind the now stopped car.

In the seconds that followed, people ran from every direction. The mother first, her companion, people from other cars and from the houses nearby. The black car did not move, nor did its occupants. A man and a woman were slouched over into the airbags.

Someone called 999.

There was shouting, disorganisation, someone was doing CPR on the boy's lifeless body and there was blood. There was a lot of blood. On the boy, on people's hands, on the road, inside the car.

Soon blue lights and sirens filled the air and still, the driver and passenger did not stir. Paramedics flew to the child lying in the road. Bystanders gave them space, huddled in small groups. The mother, comforted by her friend. Traffic police, taking photographs, taking statements and speaking into their radios.

And then, another scream. This time, from inside the car. Another female voice, screaming and screaming and flailing arms and more screaming as she tried to get out of the passenger door.

The boy's body was carried on a stretcher to the back of the ambulance and a second one careered around the corner. There was noise and flashing lights and then there was silence in the evening light.

Two ambulances, a fire and rescue team, three police cars filled the small street.

Chapter 1

2017

Her phone bounced along the desk as yet another message came through. He was relentless tonight and she still had reports to finish and an application to write before tomorrow's deadline. She couldn't afford to get distracted. She ignored the next four messages that came through. Even without turning over her phone, she knew that there would be at least two picture messages and that was something that she could not see — not now. She gritted her teeth and steeled herself back into a determined state of concentration. Within seconds of her resolve, three more messages saw her phone judder across the desk towards her once again, begging her to pick it up and reply.

"Argh!" she gave in. "Why? Why tonight?" she groaned into the balls of her hands.

She was exhausted after the longest week of her career and at, looking at the clock, 9 p.m., she still had about three hours work to do.

As the phone began to vibrate once again she grabbed it and headed to the kitchen. Switching on the kettle, she grabbed a mug and a teabag and unlocked her phone. She knew this was dangerous. She reminded herself about the application deadline tomorrow and dramatically told that she could be risking her career progression by doing this, but she couldn't help it. He made her feel so good about herself.

Hello beautiful

Are you busy?

I guess you are…

He'd sent her a photo of his face, handsome as ever, clear blue sparkling eyes and dirty blond hair staring up at her. Her heart did a mild flip in her chest and her stomach knotted as it always did when he threw those sexy eyes at her.

I miss you (heart emoji)

Do you miss me???

I know you can hear your phone. It's probably right in front of you.

Just one teeny tiny text??

Followed as predicted by another picture, a glass of red wine.

Want to join me for a glass?

She noticed that as soon as she opened the messages, he was online and typing again.

Ah-ha! Got your attention didn't I?

It was the photo messages wasn't it?

You expected something else, maybe?

Unlike her, he wrote his messages in several short sentences, pressing send after each one. She preferred to get all her thoughts down before pressing send. He'd told her many times that this was frustrating, he could see that she was typing but had to wait. Lucy had reminded him that instant gratification isn't good for the soul and that modern technology and social media thrived on our need to be instantly gratified. Although, so did Amazon Prime, which, unashamedly, she used a lot.

She typed quickly, one handed as she made herself a brew with the other,

I am working really hard to finish my work before midnight Alex, please let me. It's very important to me. I promise I am all yours tomorrow. Lx

Pocketing her phone knowing that he'd see the message and would sulk at her lack of neediness, she headed back to the table in the lounge where her papers were laid out in untidy piles.

Her phone indicated another message.

:(

Come over when you finish, I miss you too much.

She smiled, kissed her phone, replied 'OK' and put it onto silent. She would get this work finished by midnight if it killed her and he could wait up for her if he so wished.

Lucy had been working at the school for six years and had slowly worked her way up from the fresh-out-of-uni, newly qualified teacher at 22 years of age to top of the pay scale; from very little responsibility beyond teaching her own class, to managing three subjects and applying for a place on the senior leadership team at the age of 28. Since her teenage years, she'd known what she wanted in life and had been career driven. It really hadn't taken her long to find her feet and make an impact in the small leafy suburb school, The Meadows. It had been the first school she'd applied to and they had seen her potential, snapping her up before anyone else could. She was happy with that. It was close to home and had a good reputation for its quality of education and its results.

She had been teaching for almost five years when she first met Alex. He was younger than her by a year and hadn't fully decided what he wanted to do with life. But given his drive and determination, he was still making his way up through the education system and at 27, he had a masters, a PhD and was working his way through all the letters of the alphabet (or so she joked). He would get whatever job he wanted, she was sure. As it was, in between his studies, he worked for a computer software company and made a pretty decent wage considering this job was, as he put it, a stop gap to his 'dream job' whatever that was. She marvelled at his intelligence at times and to be quite frank, it was a massive turn on. When he needed to concentrate on his studies, she let him. He, on the other hand, text her a lot. She loved it, but tonight it took all her inner strength not to pack away her laptop and drive the short distance to his.

***

They'd bumped into each other, rather dramatically, in Costa one day. Ending with her being covered in cappuccino as he swung his laptop bag over his shoulder at the same time that she walked absentmindedly behind him. He had turned to apologise and had gotten a great look at her suddenly transparent and now coffee stained blouse sticking to her balconette bra as she winced at the heat of the coffee on her skin.

Apologising with such genuine care, he had helped her into a chair, taken her bags from her arms and handed her a handful of napkins to dry herself off. Once he had been satisfied that she wasn't burnt, or injured in any way other than her pride, he had replaced her spilt coffee with a new one and added a cinnamon roll to her order. Cheekily he had bought himself the same in the hopes of getting to sit with her for a while. Once she got over the irritation that her favourite blouse was most likely ruined, and she had succumbed to the fact that his young eyes kept darting to her exposed bra and cleavage, they had talked and she was surprised that they actually had a lot in common.

The talk moved from the mundane chitter chatter to telling each other about their lives and current state of affairs as they grew more comfortable with each other. Both of them had lived this part of Lancashire all their lives. Both enjoyed the outdoors, walking, rambling, riding, and climbing. There were things they had in common and things they didn't. She'd had horses for years as a teen and had evented before teaching took over her free time, he was terrified of them; he preferred rocks, often spending days out in the wild tackling difficult climbs then camping close by, she preferred to rely on her own two feet and not a rope, she liked a warm place to sleep with electricity and hot water on tap. But despite those differences, both of them wanted to really make something of themselves. Climb the career ladder. Live a life that wanted for nothing. How it came into conversation, she couldn't recall but it was established that they were both single and mutually agreed that if they saw each other again, she would steer clear of his laptop bag, and he would buy her coffee even if he couldn't see her bra through a wet blouse. She grimaced at that one. He certainly was not shy with his words.

***

Lucy yawned, stretched her arms up above her head, arched her back and felt the bones crack and muscles complain. She'd really focussed for the last hour and a half and had finished writing her end of term reports and had made a start on her application. Exhausted she closed her laptop and stored it away in its case. The rest could wait until tomorrow in school where she could check what she'd written with her colleague, Penny, and finish it off in company of the only person she trusted to help her. The head teacher had assured her it was more a formality to hold her application on file, but being the perfectionist that she was, Lucy wouldn't hand in anything less than her best. Penny had been at the school for about 10 years longer than her and had become Lucy's classroom neighbour, friend and surrogate teacher mummy well within the first half term. It was Penny who knew everything about Lucy's life, who had giggled about the Costa incident, who made sure Lucy didn't work herself into the ground by ensuring that they watched at least one episode of friends a day on their lunchbreak as they marked books, she'd checked in on Lucy when her last boyfriend had dumped her and left her with a broken heart and who was now keen to know the details about her new 'friend' Alex.

Lucy pottered around gathering things that she needed and piling them into an overnight bag, phone in hand. It rang once before he picked up, "I'm done," she sighed wearily. "Done, done and done in."

She heard him smile, "I'm about to get into bed, want to join me?"

"Already putting my things together, I'll see you in ten. Leave the door on the latch." She hung up and threw the phone into her overnight bag, picked up her work bag and headed for the door, humming. She flipped off the light and stepped into the porch. It was 10:49 pm.

As she stepped through the door and turned to lock it, she felt something hard hit her head, pain seared and she dropped her bags to bring her hands to her head. Another thud reverberated through her skull and she blacked out.

***

She was aware that she was lying down, but she was confused. Her cheek was pressed against something cold and hard. She wasn't in her bed. Was she outside? She could hear rustling. What happened? She was shivering, her head was throbbing, her throat was dry and her face felt wet, as if she had been crying.

"Lucy?" His voice cut through the darkness. He sounded panicked. She heard his feet running, no, she felt his feet running. What was going on? She couldn't see much in the darkness. "Shit, Lucy. Stay still.' Alex shone his phone torch in her direction. "Stay still, I'm calling 999."

999? Why? She made a move to sit up but when she tried to move her hand to push up from the ground, pain shot through her and she cried out.

"Stay still Lucy," he was sat next to her now, "I'm here now." He took off his coat and lay it over her. "Ambulance please, and police," he spoke into the phone. Lucy was aware of the concern in his voice before she was aware of the vomit in her mouth. She retched again as Alex told the operator

13

that his girlfriend had been attacked on her doorstop and that it looked like her house had been ransacked. "Yes I'm with her now… yes, yes, her face and her head are covered in blood, her arms too…" his voice continued in like a soundtrack blended into the background as he tried to think.

Blood? That was why her face felt wet. Her arms too, the pain. What the hell had happened to her? She remembered finishing her school reports, it was late, was she going to Alex's house this late? She couldn't remember much, she'd picked up her bags and was heading to the car. Then nothing. She couldn't remember anything.

"Alex?" her voice was groggy. He wasn't listening, her throat hurt, she was too quiet. "Alex?" she tried again. He looked at her.

"It's okay sweetheart," he stroked her hair, she liked it when he dragged his fingers through her curls, but that didn't happen, his hand stopped dead. He shone his torch at her hair. "There is an awful lot of blood in her hair. It's still warm, I think she's still bleeding." He spoke into the phone with a hint of something, panic? "Okay," he took off his sweater and folded it into half and half again. He pressed it to the head, hard.

The pain resonated through her body. She felt as though she was falling backwards, everything spun and she blacked out.

Lights. Voices. Crunching gravel. Nothing.

Movement. Pain. Vomit. Nothing.

Warmth. A hand on hers. She tried to speak through dry lips. No sound came. Her eyes felt heavy, but she forced them open. The room flickered and danced into focus. There was a fluorescent light coming from somewhere, dulled by a curtain around her and beeps from somewhere further away. Was she in hospital? A noise came from her left side and she moved her eyes that way. Alex was hunched over the bed, asleep, holding her hand. He looked so peaceful and yet there was concern etched all over his face, his brow furrowed and the skin around his eyes was puffy. She tried to speak again and when there was barely an audible whisper, she wiggled her fingers hoping to get his attention.

His head shot up and he shook the blonde waves of hair from his face. Man, he looked rough. His eyes were red, panicked and then, as he caught sight of her awake a tear escaped and rolled down his cheek. Brushing it away with the back of his hand, he stood up and leant over her. "You scared the hell out of me." He kissed her cheeks and her mouth, tenderly, his tears falling once again. "I'll let the nurses know you are awake."

"Not yet," she whispered before starting to cry. "What happened?"

"Oh Lucy, can't you remember?"

She shook her head as best she could. "I was coming to you, the last thing I remember was leaving the house.

He dragged the chair closer to her head and sat back down, leaning in to wipe the tears from her eyes.

"Did I crash? Did I hurt anyone? I was really tired, it was probably my fault."

"No, no, Lucy! You didn't even get out of your porch."

She was looking at his face. He looked in pain and she wondered how he had known she was here.

"How..?"

A nurse bustled in through the curtain and did a double take, "You're awake!" she smiled. "Your boyfriend was under strict instructions to let us know the minute you woke up," she winked at Alex and looked at Lucy, "He's been here since you arrived, you know. Hasn't left your side."

Lucy smiled and tried to turn her head to look at him.

"Are you in pain Lucy?" the nurse asked.

"Yeah," croaked Lucy "...my head," she paused, "and my arm feels like it's been put on backwards." She saw Alex swallow and look down at the floor.

"I will get you some more pain relief in that," she nodded at Lucy's hand where she saw a needle and tubes that led to a drip hanging above the bed. "Get you more comfortable, eh?"

Lucy gave a weak smile and the nurse left the bay.

16

Another drip bag was hung, some pain relief injected into the cannula in her hand and soon, she was drifting back off to sleep.

Chapter 2

She was standing in a doorway. There was a movement in the blackness in front of her and then pain. So much pain. She screamed out, in fear, arms flailing in front of her.

"Lucy! Lucy, wake up." Alex was stilling her arms and then stroking her face.

It had been a week since she'd been discharged from the hospital; referred to the fracture clinic for her arm and to the outpatient's department for her stitches, all 25 of them. She had lost count of the number of times this nightmare had woken her in the night. Her right arm was broken in three places, she had a couple of broken ribs and she was lucky to still have her right eye, the 8 stitches above her eye socket were testament to that. The most serious of her injuries was to her head. She was extremely lucky that she hadn't needed surgery to release pressure from the swelling inside her skull, they'd even considered inducing a coma at one point. It hadn't been necessary – her body had kept her asleep for almost three days before she had opened her eyes. She was lucky but she's still had a massive wound and it had taken hours of surgery and then 17 stitches to close the gaping hole in her skull. Her body felt as though she'd fallen from a horse and been body-slammed into a solid cross-country fence. That, she wouldn't have minded. The truth wasn't that easy to accept.

She had been attacked. Viciously attacked in her own doorway and left for dead in her porch. She had been leaving to go to Alex's house and someone had taken a golf club to her. It looked as though she had tried to protect herself by lifting her hands to cover her face after the first blow before spinning around and falling to the ground where the bastard had continued to beat her before taking the golf club into her house and smashing everything to pieces. Nothing taken but everything destroyed.

Lucy was asked by the police if there had been any grievances - she couldn't think of anything, not at work, within the family or in the neighbourhood. They then asked her if there had been anything valuable in the house that had been the topic of dispute – again, not that she could think of, she didn't own many things of monetary value. The police had then shown her photographs of the living room, which had been trashed, cabinets overturned, table and chairs upended and the glass coffee table smashed. Everything she held valuable could be seen in those photos, the TV (albeit smashed) the painting that she'd bought at auction just after her graduation was hanging lopsided on the wall and her laptop had been in her bag. Nothing had been taken by the looks of it. Nothing physical at all.

What had been taken was far more upsetting. Her freedom, her courage and her sanity. She moved back in with her mum while the landlord claimed on the insurance and carried out the essential repairs. But after a day being in the house alone when her mum went to work, Lucy soon realised that she could not bear to be alone. She was scared of everything. Freaking out at every little noise, screaming in terror when the postman pushed a letter through the letterbox making her jump, and even the rain on the window sent her heart into a state of panic.

Alex had suggested, as he worked and studied at home, that she move into his flat with him for the time being and so she did. She was still paying rent on the house, even though she hadn't stepped foot through the door since the night of the attack. She didn't know if she ever would.

With time her arm healed and the cast taken off, her cuts on her face and her head scabbed and started to fade, even her hair started to grow back where they'd shaved it for surgery. The police had been unable to find any CCTV, dash-cam footage and there were no witnesses or anybody seen hanging around. As unfortunate as it was, the attack appeared to have been random and they were sure that she was not personally in any danger.

Standing in the bedroom ironing a few weeks later, she inhaled the scent of hot cotton and steam and smiled. It was a Sunday night, and she was getting her clothes for returning to school the next day. She was ready for this. She needed to regain a little bit of herself again. Damn it, she needed routine and 'normality' back. Doing very little for the last seven weeks had been nice to begin with, but then the days had started to drag and she got bored. Alex's flat had never been so clean and tidy. She had rearranged the kitchen cupboards, under the stairs, the messy drawer and to be quite frank she thought he might be glad that she was going back to marking books and planning lessons, he might be able to find his belongings again. She laughed to herself.

He coughed at the bedroom door to alert her to his presence, not that she needed those small gestures anymore. He walked up behind her resting his chin on her shoulder, "How are you feeling?"

"I don't know," she laughed, "Nervous that people will talk about me behind my back?"

"Nah, they've done that for weeks – out of the system by now," he joked then asked seriously, "What about teaching? You feel like you've still got your hand in?"

"I haven't really missed any work, have I? It's been the summer holidays mostly." She stood the iron up and hung her skirt on the hanger.

"I guess," he spun her around and looked into her eyes. "I just want you to know that you don't have to, you know, if you don't want to…"

"You're going to miss me," she teased kissing him on the nose.

"I am," he nodded his agreement. "Who else is going to supply me with cups of coffee all day long?" he mocked angst and she laughed. She knew he was worried that she wasn't emotionally ready to go back to work and his fears weren't totally unfounded. But at some point, she just had to take that leap of faith. Penny had visited her a lot over the summer and was picking her up in the morning. Everything would fall into place the second she walked through those double doors and became Miss Lawrence again. She hoped she was right.

"Ooh, are you wearing that blouse?" he looked over her to get a better look at the white blouse hanging over the wardrobe door, "I remember that blouse," he winked at her.

"It's my favourite, I don't think we would be together now if the coffee stain hadn't come out of it," she shot him a warning glance but couldn't keep serious. He wasn't even listening, he was grinning like a naughty school boy. "Hey!" she shook him back to reality.

"Sorry," he smirked, "I was reliving a moment." He cupped his hands around her face and kissed her nose, her cheeks, her eyelids and then, finally, her mouth. "The moment I fell in love…"

"Yeah," she whispered, "with my tits!"

"It's where it started, I can't deny that." He bent down and kissed each breast through her strappy pyjama top. "See, they love me too." He moved a hand from where it rested, just above her hip up to her chest and ran his index finger in circles around each erect nipple. She let out a soft breath and, taking encouragement, he captured her right nipple between his thumb and finger and squeezed it gently. She closed her eyes and exhaled. God, he loved this woman, she was beautiful.

He slowly lifted the hem of her top and she raised her arms above her head allowing him to take it off and look at her. Her pale skin, dark nipples, dark hair curling down to rest on her shoulder. Her green eyes, her perfect cupid bow lips. He was one lucky, lucky guy. He dragged his t-shirt over his head and pulled her close, soaking in her scent and feeling her kiss his chest, working her way along his collar bone and up his neck until she met his mouth. The chemistry between them was insane, it always had been since the first time they were alone together and still, now. He had never felt this way about anyone, ever. She was unbuttoning his jeans and sliding her hands down to his bum. She grabbed his buttocks in her hands and groaned into his mouth enjoying what she was feeling press against her. He lifted her easily, her legs wrapped around his waist and placed her onto the bed pulling her pyjama bottoms from the ankles. Then he was on top of her again. Kissing her breasts, down between her ribcage, down to her stomach and then, lower. She reached down and ran her fingers through his hair as he kissed the insides of her thighs. His kisses made her stomach twist in delight as his lips moved further up, tantalisingly slow and tender until he was kissing her there, right on that sweet, spot through her knickers.

The heat surged through her body, every nerve tingling, yearning for him. She moaned and urgently, he pulled at the final few buttons of his jeans so that he could remove them in one swift movement without leaving her longing for him for more than a second. As he did so, she wriggled her hips and slipped her knickers down and off. He was hungry for her and she was already pulling him closer down on top of her, kissing him, spreading her legs, lifting her hips in anticipation. He didn't need asking twice and in one thrust he took her. Her intake of breath telling him everything he needed to know. They made love urgently and yet tenderly. Him allowing her to climax and call out his name in ecstasy more than once before he thrust his way to his own demise.

Afterwards stroking her sides and kissing the top of her head as she slept, he couldn't imagine life without her. He'd almost lost her. The night of the attack.

She had called him around ten to eleven which was the latest she had ever agreed to come over. The drive took around 12 minutes in clear traffic and about 20 minutes at busier times. He kept an eye on the time until 11 p.m. and then had filled the kettle, retrieved two mugs from the cupboard and prepped cups of tea for them both. He'd then pottered around, getting the kitchen spotless and had decided to put bread in the toaster, just in case. Half expecting her to knock on the door half way through all of this, he hadn't looked at his watch since and was shocked to see that it was 11:15 p.m. when he suddenly caught sight of the oven clock. He wandered into the living room to check his phone. No missed call, no message, just the sweet selfie of them both on the screen. He hit redial and waited for her to pick up. She hadn't.

He'd waited until 11:30, having tried her phone several times, he began to panic and had grabbed his coat and keys and ran out of the flat. Lucy was never late for anything. Never. He tried not to imagine her car lying at the side of the road, but it was the only possible reason that she hadn't made it to his. The roads were twisting and narrow and, even in good conditions, were a hazard if a car didn't dip its lights in time. Every turn in the road heard him release sigh of relief when he saw no blue Clio overturned in the road. Where the hell was she?

As he turned into her street, he grinned and shook his head, she hadn't left yet? What had she found that needing doing at this time of night? Or had she fallen asleep on the sofa as she called him? He parked up and walked around the front of the car to her driveway. Something wasn't right. Her front door was open and what was that on the floor? He had screamed out her name when he realised it was her and he'd run towards her. She was cold and lifeless and he genuinely thought she was dead. It wasn't until he shone his torch on her face and saw the colour on her lips that he knew she was still alive. He'd called 999 and waited the most agonising eight and a half minutes until the first responder and then the paramedics had arrived. A police officer had travelled in the ambulance with her and he had been taken to the local police station to make a statement and to give any information that may help their investigation. There had been so much blood. Someone had wanted to kill her. They'd almost succeeded.

The doctors had suggested a golf club as the weapon and judging by the shape of the dent in her skull, an iron of some sort. Alex had paced the corridor the entire time she was in surgery. Fragments of her skull being dug out of the soft tissue. He overheard the doctors saying that they had never seen such a mess. Commenting on how they were amazed she hadn't been killed with any one of the blows. He had walked out of the hospital at that point and screamed at the sky. A harrowing, heart-breaking cry. He did not understand how anyone could do this to Lucy. Lucy, the kindest, most loving and generous person on the planet.

After he had been questioned and had made his statement, Alex had been allowed to go to the hospital to see Lucy. She was in theatre when he got there and he used her phone to call her mum, Maggie, who had arrived with a flask long before Lucy was out of theatre. There were police everywhere. Talking to the medical staff and taking verbal updates, reporting back to the station and the other investigating officers. Alex couldn't get his head around it. It simply wasn't possible for anyone to hold so much hatred towards Lucy that would cause them to smash her skull in. End of.

Lying on the bed, her warmth radiating around him, he knew she was lucky to be alive and that meant that he was the lucky to get to call her his own. He promised himself in that moment that he would protect her forever. He just wasn't sure how he would get through the day when was at work tomorrow. He rolled onto his side, made sure the quilt cover was tucked around her shoulders and gazed at her beauty in the dim glow of the streetlight outside the window.

***

Her first day back at work had been challenging. Not in a bad way, in a relentless, how-many-things-to-do sort of a way. The usual ruthless teacher day where you can't switch off from the second the children arrive until they leave at the end of the day. She had loved it. But she also couldn't wait to get home and have a bath. At 3:32 her mobile rang.

"Hi," she smiled, "It's almost as if you knew I needed to hear your voice."

"So, Miss Lawrence, how did it go?"

"Great! I'm tired and need a long soak in the bath, but I've loved being back." She pottered around her classroom putting books back on the shelves and pencils back in pots.

"So, you didn't miss daytime TV?" he was teasing her now.

"Nope."

"And you didn't miss our elevenses?" she heard the intonation in his voice and knew that he had just raised his eyebrows. She flushed remembering those lazy, long summers' days after her recovery where they had enjoyed the excitement of living together and seeing *a lot* of each other on a regular basis.

"Hmmm," she wrinkled her nose and smiled, "Maybe."

Changing the subject, he asked, "What would you like for dinner? I can make food whilst you relax in the bath?"

"There's an offer I will not refuse!" she laughed, "Erm, I fancy Greek food."

"Sounds like a plan. Moussaka?"

"Oh yum," she heard her stomach rumble at the thought.

"I'll get started on it when I finish up for the day. Oh, and the guys were asking if we wanted to climb this weekend. I said I'd check with you first, have a think and let me know."

Lucy glanced at the classroom door when she caught sight of someone standing there, waiting. She mouthed 'hi' and then spoke into the phone "Gary has popped over to see me, I'll text when I know what time we're leaving."

"Oh, can't keep the head waiting. Go, go. Love you."

"Loves back," she blew a kiss into the phone and hung up.

Gary came into the classroom and perched on the front table. "The day went well?" he tilted his head sympathetically.

"It did," she beamed. "I've missed the non-stop buzz of the children, although," she massaged the back of her neck, "I can feel the start of a headache."

"Ah, that will be caffeine withdrawals, you will have drank less coffee than you've been used to at home." he smiled at her. "I just wanted to check on you, I know you will have been the brilliant teacher you always were, but it's the rest of the job, the bit that no one sees." Nodding towards her desk and her pile of marking, "You let me know if it all gets too much, the offer of phased return is still there, if you need it."

She smiled, she had a good support network here and Gary was a great head teacher, really cared about his staff. "I'll let you know if it gets too much," she promised.

He took one last look around the classroom, smiled again and left.

"First day, done," she muttered and headed for the desk and the three sets of books, two of which she should have marked at lunchtime but had been too busy catching up with Penny about how living with Alex was going.

At about 4:45, Lucy text Alex to say that she was on her way home and he sent a photo back of dinner preparations. *YUM!* She messaged back. If there was one thing Lucy loved about living with Alex was that when he made meals, he really made meals. She knew for sure that when dinner was served tonight, it would be an all-out Greek feast. He text back straight away to let her know that the bath was running. Bliss. She was onto a winner here.

Chapter 3

After their initial meeting, Lucy had perhaps - no definitely, spent more time in Costa. There was something about Alex that she couldn't put her finger on. He'd really put a spell on her. Sitting at the corner table, she felt daft the first time she'd nonchalantly headed in for a coffee and 'work.' She'd taken her laptop to make her feel less conspicuous sat on her own, yet she felt self-conscious in the corner tap-tapping away. Plus, her mind wasn't really on the job. Every time the door opened, her heart would flutter a little and she'd try to look up without looking desperate.

He didn't return for coffee in the first week, nor the second. She was spending a fortune on coffee and cake and thus, had increased her hours at the gym to counteract the calories. Damn it, by this point, she hoped he *was* as good looking and charismatic as she recalled. She hoped he was worth this effort! The staff knew her by name and what she drank, she no longer felt stupid sitting doing her work – hell, she even knew where the plug sockets were and which table had the best light. She had to admit that working in Costa had become her favourite place, nobody could come past her classroom and ask a favour but equally, she had 'left the building' and boy did that feel good some evenings.

The warmth of the evening air blew in her direction in the May as she sat with a coffee browsing for the girly holiday she and Penny were desperate to book when, she became aware of a presence to her left and then a tray slid onto the table in front of her.

"Is this seat taken?" his voice reverberated right through her pelvic region. She tried to calm her face and her heart rate before turning around to see his friendly smile. "I do believe I promised to buy you coffee. You're not leaving anytime soon?" he cocked his head towards the tray laden with cake and coffee.

She looked at her watch, "Nope," she grinned trying not to look too keen, "I don't have to leave just yet." She closed the laptop and stored it away in her bag under the table. She didn't trust her nerves not to spill coffee all over it.

"Good news for me then!" he sat down opposite, passing her a coffee and sliding a plate of cake in her direction. "I'm in need of female company," he chuckled to himself, "After three weeks in a tent full of lads," he sniffed his shirt, "I have never been so glad to see my shower."

Lucy raised her eyebrow in a questioning manner, what was he on about?

"Climbing holiday in France." He took a sip of his coffee. "Four lads, one tent, lots of climbing and lots of wine." He looked her in the face, "Lack of female company, showers and any kind of civilised way of living."

She wrinkled her nose and shook her head. "Sounds," she paused, "fun?"

"Great climbing. Ticked off some good routes."

She must have looked puzzled so he continued, "Every year we head over to Fontainbleau and spend a few weeks making the most of the weather before it gets too warm."

She knew that he must be wondering if she even recalled their first conversations and almost blushed at the realisation that she could recall everything he had told her. Hell, she'd replayed that evening over and over in her head a million times. "Too warm? You can never be 'too warm' on holiday! I was just planning a holiday for a girl's week away. The hotter the better!" She smiled, "Man, I need a holiday!"

He, also recalling their first conversation, couldn't imagine Lucy in a tent. No, she was an all-inclusive, 5 star, plenty of sun loungers and big swimming pools kind of girl. He tried not to imaging her in a bikini – which of course he then did and got a semi, much to his annoyance. She was beautiful. He watched her mouth as she ate her cake. He wanted to kiss that perfect mouth. He grinned at her.

"What are you grinning at?"

"Just wondering if it's rude that I wish your blouse was stuck to your chest again," her eyes widened, he froze realising what he had just uttered, "Um, that was crass, sorry. That's what too much time with the lads will do to you. Forgive me?" His eyes twinkled with a boyish amusement. She tutted and smacked the back of his hand with her fingers noticing the electricity that passed between them. He felt it too, she noticed his cheeks warm and reluctantly stowed her hand back under the table not unaware of her heart pounding out of her chest and a warm sensation filling her lower belly.

"I, um -"

"Can I have your number, Lucy?"

She nodded, unable to speak in the moment.

"I am just so bloody glad you were here this evening, I was hoping you would be."

He was honest, she thought. She would not be telling him how much time and money she'd spent here in the last month hoping that he would pop by. They drank their drinks, ate their cakes and when it was time to leave, he walked her back to the car. After she'd put her bags on the back seat, she closed the car door and turned around to face him. He was closer than she realised and her breath caught in her chest for a second.

"It was nice to see you again, Lucy," his mouth was twitching up into a smile at the edges.

Her heart was pounding, "You still want my number?" she asked.

He nodded, glad that she had brought it up, no one needs to feel desperate enough to have to ask twice. He handed her his phone so that she could call herself and share his number with her. And then, he took one step closer and kissed her on the cheek.

Well, she could have died there and then, her heart certainly missed at least three beats before making up for it with a heartrate worthy of cardiac exercise. Had she not been brought up so well, it would have been very, very easy for her to invite him back to her house. She didn't know what it was about him, but she really liked him and those eyes, that smile... She didn't invite him back, instead she smiled, climbed into the driver's seat and started the engine.

On the short drive home, she had kicked herself for not reciprocating his kiss. She wound down the window and, catching sight of herself in the mirror, told herself, "Grow up girl."

***

Alex met her in the hallway to take her coat and school bags, kissed her and ushered her up to the bathroom with the promise that wine would be following in just a few minutes and now, sinking into the bubbles and hot water, she felt the tension of the day leave her. Her toes, nails painted pink, peeped out of the water near the taps and her chin sunk under the water ever so slightly because she wasn't quite tall enough to reach both ends of the bath. A polite knock at the door and Alex came in carrying two glasses of white wine. She smiled and nodded at the side of the bath, where he placed her glass before sitting himself on the toilet seat.

"You're grinning," she noted catching his eye.

"You're naked," he grinned even more, if that was possible.

"And?"

"And, I may have missed you a teeny bit today. I got used to having you around," he shrugged. "Maybe I'm just addicted to you." He took a sip of his wine and then knelt on the floor next to her, leant over the bath and kissed her.

"There are worse things to be addicted to," she mused.

They shared a few minutes of comfortable quiet before Alex smiled, "I'd better check on dinner, I'll let you relax."

She had some wine and lay back in the hot bubbles, praising herself for how well she had done today. She was as confident as always in the classroom. The only time she had jumped was on the way home in Penny's car when a bicycle had caught her off guard as it passed the passenger window. She had jumped and yelped like an injured puppy but Penny had quickly soothed her with her calm and collected rational thoughts. Things like this irked her, there were trauma responses but there were also stupid irrational flight actions and, as much as Penny reassured her it was normal to have reactions to things, they really irritated Lucy and she wished she could just go back to how she had been before; confident and free of all care. Even now, she felt her heartrate quicken irrationally, she closed her eyes and counted back from ten, breathing in through her nose and out through her mouth as she did. Her online, self-help therapy sessions (thank you YouTube) had certainly proved their usefulness.

After her bath and a delicious dinner of moussaka, flat bread and olives. She sighed a happy sort of sigh and headed for the sofa whilst Alex loaded the dishwasher. She glanced at the picture over the fireplace. A photograph taken on one of his climbing holidays a few years earlier. It had been printed on a canvas; stone steps leading through the forest with the sun's rays streaming through onto a huge rock. It was oozed sentimental value for him, reminding him of the weeks of climbing just south of Paris. He had told her about his love for climbing early the very first time they'd met and she loved his passion for it – a similar passion to that of hers and teaching. She lay, smiling at the picture, snuggled into the cushions until he came back into the room. They sat, comfortable in each other's' company; her feet in his lap, their hands entwined, until she started to fall asleep and decided that bed was the better place to be.

Three weeks back at work and Lucy was back to her organised, creative and fun-loving self. Her class this year were harder work than she was used to, but she was turning them around. Another four weeks and she was ready for the October half term. She had a cold and her head hurt from the inside. End-of-term-itus she called it – her body knew it was about to get a week off and the illnesses were creeping in a few days early. Alex had only moaned once about the amount of Vaporub she was using but when she offered to sleep on the sofa, he quickly reassured her that he could cope.

On the last day of term, Lucy and Penny were waiting with their classes at the door at the end of the day. It was overcast and Lucy was waiting for parents to come and collect the last few children. "Another ten minutes and we're FREE!" she joked to Penny. When Penny didn't respond, Lucy nudged her, "What's up?"

Penny turned to face Lucy, "Look behind me, at the gate, red car."

Lucy looked over Penny's shoulder towards the car, standing next to it was a man in a black jacket and he was staring at them, his face did not look friendly. Lucy shuddered. Another man joined him, looked towards the two teachers, nodded and pointed menacingly before walking around to the passenger side and getting in. The driver kept looking at them until he was in the car and driving off.

"What was that about?" asked Lucy.

"Not sure," Penny ushered Lucy inside, "But they weren't happy about something."

"Gave me the creeps." Lucy pulled her cardigan around her. "We should let Gary know. Just in case." Penny nodded and they headed off in the direction of the headteacher's office.

Half term bliss. No alarms set. Breakfast at a more normal time and long lazy days with Alex, she could think of nothing better. Alex was taking her climbing today. There was a local centre that he had taken her to on a couple of occasions in the early stages of their relationship, it was possibly only their second or third casual date. She wasn't much into sports which could damage you, but the centre sold good coffee and even better, the tastiest muffins. Sitting in the café area reminded her of when they'd met and on the plus side, she got to watch *him* climb and *that* was a treat. Especially when he got all hot and needed to take his shirt off (although how taking his shirt off helped, she didn't know, she was convinced it was all for her benefit). He had the most beautifully sculpted body. Honestly, she had seen nothing like it, ever. Sleek, toned muscles moving across the wall from one hold to the next. She had never wanted anyone more than she wanted him right then. She wished she had the nerve to tell him so.

***

The very first time he had taken her to the climbing wall, he'd asked her what she thought.

"It was - hot, in there," she tried to sound as normal as possible but she was nervous.

"Lots of bodies all crushing routes," he nodded, eyes firmly on the road.

"No, I meant," she paused, "Hot, hot."

He looked at her, saw her flushing and realised what sort of hot she meant. "You liked?"

"Are you asking if I liked the look of you semi-naked, hanging from a wall?"

"I guess I am,"

"Well, then, yes. I did. There was something primitive about it."

"Did it turn you on?" He was smiling, staring straight ahead at the road, she was blushing and suddenly finding her bra too tight to get a deep breath.

They had been dating for just over a month at this point and so far, there had been very little physical contact other than kissing and holding hands – her grandmother would have been proud of her. Alex hadn't asked or assumed anything and she admired the respect he had for her. But, seeing his bare chest today had given her the first glimpse of what she could have if she wanted it, which she did.

"Maybe," her voice sounded breathy and she instantly realised that she had just opened a door to another level of their relationship. Her palms grew sweaty, felt her heartrate increase and an unexpected twinge in her groin.

When the car had pulled up outside her house, instead of leaning over for a kiss like he would usually have done, he sat with both hands on the wheel of the car, staring straight in front.

"Are you coming in?" she asked him, wondering what he was thinking.

"Only if you're sure you want me to?"

She opened her door and stepped out. "I am inviting you in." She walked around the back of the car, up the drive and into the house. She left the door ajar. Once inside, her heartrate picked up as she craned her ear to gauge if he was going to join her or not. It took him a little more than 30 seconds. But she heard the car door open and close, the click of him locking it, then his steps on the gravel walking towards the house. Shit, this was really happening. She wondered where, how, when. If she was already a fumbling mess in her head, how the hell was she going to be able to do this in reality? She had just thrown her bag onto the armchair and her coat on top of it when she heard the door shut. She froze, feeling his presence right behind her. He lifted her hair at the back of her neck and kissed her.

"You smell beautiful." He put his hands on her waist and spun her around to face him.

Her breath shuddered out between her lips when she saw the intensity in his eyes. Her heart was now pounding around inside her chest so ferociously that she was sure he could hear it. He reached out and placed his hands either side of her face and kissed her. Unlike any of their kisses before, there was a hunger that grew, an anticipation for more, this time. Catching her breath between kisses, she started to lead him towards the stairs and he followed willingly, turned on with her taking the lead. At the top of the stairs, she kicked off her pumps and headed for the bedroom; never before had she felt so sexy.

The next two hours were possibly the best two hours of her existence thus far. He made her feel like a goddess in the way he looked at her, the way her caressed her body, in the way that he took time to give *her* pleasure. It had never been like this before. A quick fumble at best with the three guys she'd been with and always for the guy's pleasure. But this, *this* was magical. Every nerve ending in her body sang out for more. This was how it was meant to be, the connection, the energy, the confidence she had. He knew what he was doing and how to give her what she needed. And when he had brought her to orgasm he let her revel in the feeling of utter contentment before starting over again, and again. He only took pleasure for himself after she was spent and too exhausted for more. Afterwards they had lay, half wrapped in the bedsheets, gazing at each other. Both amazed at how good their first time together had been. There had been no awkwardness. It was like it was meant to be, they were meant to be. Alex felt the same and wanted to tell her there and then that he would worship the ground she walked on forever, but had shivered at how cheesy it sounded. Instead he kissed each of her fingers, her eyes, her nose and her mouth before closing his own eyes and reliving the best moments from their evening together.

Chapter 4

It was the Saturday afternoon and the first day of her half term break. They'd enjoyed a few hours of climbing and then catching up with their friends over a coffee and muffin. Still covered in chalk dust, they stopped off at the local supermarket to pick up bits for dinner. Lucy was wandering through the frozen section when she was suddenly aware of a presence behind her, "Alex," she smiled and turned around grinning.

Not Alex.

A man in a black hood stood less than an inch away. His face contorted in anger and his pupils pinpoints.

Frantically, Lucy tried to move out of his way but his tattooed fists banged down on the freezers either side of her, preventing her from moving. He stepped closer, so close that she could smell the alcohol and stale cigarette smoke on him. She started to scream but he pre-empted that and put his hand over her mouth.

"Take this, you bitch." He thrust his knee into her stomach with so much force that she was momentarily lifted into the air before crumpling into a heap on the floor. She watched his black boots walk away from her and disappeared around the corner. Closing her eyes tightly together to try and make sense of what had happened, but all she could feel were her insides, shaking uncontrollably. She wanted to be sick. She tried to scramble to her knees and crawl but winded as she was, she ended up curled in a foetal position on the floor. Tears prickled in her eyes and she squeezed them again, focussing on her breathing which was suddenly very painful.

She was aware of a trolley turning into the aisle and a woman's voice shouting, louder than Lucy could bear in that moment, "Can I get some help here?" and she raced over to kneel next to Lucy. "Are you okay love?" she asked.

"A man," Lucy gasped for air, "A man. Black hood," was all she could manage to say between breaths.

"Are you hurt?"

Lucy nodded.

"Lucy?" It was Alex's voice now. In no time at all he had run down the aisle and was on the floor with her. "What happened? Did you fall?"

"She said a man did this to her," the woman remarked.

"A man?" Fear rose in his eyes. "Did you see his face Lucy?"

She nodded.

By now, there was quite a crowd of people hovering at the ends of the aisles. The store manager had been alerted and was stood talking into his headset. "Can you check the CCTV for aisle seven please? Yes, the last five minutes, let me know." The manager leaned over to talk to Lucy and Alex, "We're checking the CCTV, see if we can get a look at who did this."

Lucy had managed to sit up now, albeit a little hunched. Her stomach muscles ached and she was shivering from the shock of the attack. A lady had passed a shawl to Lucy and it was now gratefully wrapped around her shoulders.

"What happened?" Alex was asking her.

"I thought it was you behind me," she whispered. "I turned around and he was right in my face." Big fat tears rolled down her cheek. "I tried to scream but he put his hand over my mouth and then kneed me in the stomach." Alex clenched and unclenched and then clenched his fists again. His blood was boiling, he wanted to go outside and hunt down the animal that had hurt his Lucy.

The store manager was talking to a woman in the doorway to the stock room in what looked like a heated manner. Alex noticed and excused himself from Lucy's side to see what the fuss was about. "Well?" he asked, as patiently as he could.

"It appears your lady friend here was indeed attacked by a person in a black hood."

Alex watched the lady look at the manager and then to the floor. He pressed, "And?"

"And the cameras didn't pick up his face."

"None of them?" Alex was seething now. "Not one single fucking camera got a look at him?"

"I'm very sorry sir. The police have been called and you're welcome to come and sit in the staffroom, if you wish?"

Alex stomped back over to Lucy, cursing under his breath.

Lucy preferred to wait in the car for the police and once she was out of the store and back in the car, she wept uncontrollably. Alex put his arms around her and comforted her as best he could through his rage.

"Why me? Why? What have I ever done to anyone?" she sobbed.

"I am so sorry I wasn't there." Alex was choking up as well. His girl, his beautiful girl had been hurt again and he'd been powerless to do anything about it even though he had promised her that he would always protect her.

The police arrived and took statements. Alex asked the police what they were going to do explaining that this was the second attack in a little over three months and that he was worried for the safety of his girlfriend. They had the information from the previous attack already and they explained that Lucy would need her to see a doctor in order to get a welfare check on file, to check for internal injuries, to see if she was in shock. Lucy agreed. Then they gave her the number to call if she remembered anything else. They told her that they would look at CCTV in the local area but until they could get a positive ID on the man, there was little they could do. Alex grabbed the steering wheel of the car with both hands and screamed in frustration. And once that was out of him, he breathed in and out heavily for a moment to regain his composure.

"Let's get you checked out," he glanced over at Lucy who was pale, the colour washed from her cheeks and eyes glassy from crying. He reached over to stroke her leg and winced as she jumped at his touch. He would make whoever did this, pay.

The examination by the doctor a few hours later was uncomfortable but thankfully not painful enough to make Lucy worry about lasting or threatening damage. A police officer had arrived to take a further statement from the doctor, about her injuries. Mostly there was bruising to her abdomen, internal swelling and some soft tissue damage. She was told to rest for a couple of days and to take paracetamol. She was relieved in a way that it was a minor fix, but terrified that this had happened to her, not once but twice now, the first nearly fatal. Both sudden and unexpected. Both painful.

Determined not to let it get to her and being the outwardly strong person that she was, she decided that she was incredibly unlucky and she must just have one of those faces.

Back home, in Alex's bed, he fussed over her, plumping pillows, fetching her favourite books, TV remotes, iPad, cups of tea, and so on. She really wanted for nothing – except sleep. It came quickly. The adrenaline of her ordeal on top of her aching post-climbing body ensured that she slept well.

The rest of the half term sped past. After an initial day and a half in bed, Lucy found that other than the transition from sitting to standing which used her core muscles, she was able to get on with most things. She baked some cakes, finished a jigsaw, did some reading and TV flicking whilst Alex lay in whatever room she was in, reading magazines and scrolling Facebook. Everything apart from that first weekend of the holiday had been unusually normal.

As the week drew to a close, Alex asked her once again if she felt able to return to work.

"Of course I do. Alex, I'm okay."

"But –"

"But nothing, I was in the wrong place at the wrong time and got in the way of someone's anger." She stroked his arm, "I won't let it get to me."

He let out a sigh. She was right. She was just bloody unlucky.

The remaining weeks and months of the year flew by and soon it was December. Alex was insistent on having a real tree and so, one snowy evening early on in the month, they wrapped up warm and headed out to a Christmas tree farm. Lucy revelled in the smell of pine and marvelled at the different shapes and sizes of trees. "You will need to choose," she raised her eyebrows, "I wouldn't know where to start!"

"You'll learn." He pulled her close and looked into her eyes with an intensity that made her insides quiver. He really was the most beautiful man she had ever seen and bringing her here to choose a tree for his flat, well that was pretty magical. It was even more magical when, in that very moment, it started to snow. Big snowflakes and lots of them.

Grinning like a child in her class, she had stood on her tip toes to catch a snowflake on her tongue before kissing Alex, "Now all my Christmas wishes will come true," she teased.

"Oh yeah? What wishes are those?"

"Can't tell," she winked at him, "…Won't come true if I do!" she wandered off amongst the trees, lifting her coat tails and twirling in the most girlish way possible. He laughed out loud and so, acting as childish as she felt, she darted off to hide. "Bet you can't find me!"

The snow was already gathering in the branches of the trees as she crouched behind a statue of a reindeer. She watched Alex looking for her. He was being far too grown up and serious and she felt the need for him to find his inner child. She almost giggled out loud as she waited for him to pass her and then she started throwing snowballs at him.

"What the –"

"Got ya!"

"No!" he ducked to miss the next snowball that flew his way.

She darted from her hiding place, scooping up snow as she ran and threw another snowball over her shoulder. She heard it make impact as he swore and frantically tried to gather snow. She was laughing now and was easily found by his snowball to which she retaliated with another two in quick succession. She was much better at this than he was and her glee came out in bursts of laughter floating through the pine trees.

Suddenly it was silent. She peered behind the tree to see where Alex had gone.

He had literally vanished. "Alex?"

Freezing cold ice made contact with the warmth of the nape of her neck and she screamed.

"My turn," Alex laughed from behind her.

Alex continued to laugh his boyish laugh as Lucy tried to shake the snow from inside her jumper.

"Meanie," she pouted at him.

Looking over her shoulder, he spoke softly, "Would you look at that," he sighed. "You found it."

"Found what?"

"Our tree," he smiled at her, "Look, it's just perfect." Pulling her close to him made the remaining pieces of the snowball move further down her back and she gasped. He stood behind her, lacing his hands around her waist and kissed the top of her head.

"Our tree?" she repeated his words back to him. It was *his* flat so technically *his* tree.

"Yep, yours and mine, for our first Christmas together."

She looked up at him. Beyond him, the stars twinkled in the darkness and her heart melted. She put her gloved hands either side of his face and pulled him down to her level so she could kiss him. After a few moments, he lifted her up and with her legs wrapped around his waist, they kissed again and then Lucy could contain her happiness no longer, she threw her head back and her arms out to the side and laughed. Alex laughed too and spun her around, his angel, for the top of his tree.

Chapter 5

Soon the Christmas countdown was on at school, classes were learning songs, children learning lines and there was tinsel, everywhere. Penny and Lucy had gone all out to decorate their classrooms. They had trees, stockings, advent calendars, there were cards pinned up to the displays and the glitter was not coming out of the carpet no matter how hard the cleaner tried. Teachers were busier than they had been and yet, everyone was smiling. Soon the hall was set up for the end of term Nativity. The bustle made Lucy even more excited for Christmas.

"So, have you worked out what he's planned for Christmas?" Penny quizzed her one lunchtime.

"No, but he's being super secretive about something."

"Oooh, I wonder if I need to buy a hat," she giggled.

"Don't be daft, we've not even been together a year yet," Lucy bit into her sandwich, wondering what she would say if he did ask her. She did love him. But they'd been through so much in the short time they'd been together that she wondered if it would just be his way of holding onto her a little tighter. "No, but I think he's booked something for us.

He keeps checking his emails and doesn't let me near his phone."

"I hope, whatever it is, that you love it." Penny drank the last mouthful of her tea, "You don't half deserve it," her eyes showed genuine sorrow.

"Oh get over it, will you? I'm fine."

On the last day of term, the girls were headed to their cars with their arms full of Christmas treats, Secret Santa gifts and a bottle of wine from the leadership team when Penny shouted, "I have something in my car for you, so don't go just yet."

Lucy nodded as she opened the boot of her car one handed to place her goodies inside and heard Penny totter up behind her. "I wanted to give you this. Open it now."

Lucy carefully undid the bow on the small box and gently pulled the paper from it.

"Just a little something from me to you," Penny added.

Inside the box was a set of horseshoe earrings. Lucy smiled, "They're beautiful."

"They're for luck." Penny breathed out the breath she'd been holding, "You haven't had a lot of it this year. I am hoping next year will give you more."

Lucy threw her arms around her friend and squeezed her tightly, "You are the sweetest. Here's yours." She passed over a tote bag, brimming with tissue paper. "For a bit of self-love and down-time."

"Wonderful," Penny exclaimed. "Is there a book in there too?" Lucy nodded, "Great, you always pick good ones!"

The girls hugged again, wished each other a merry Christmas and set off home.

Considering the size of the flat and the fact that only the two of them lived there, when Lucy stepped through the door there was an unusual hive of activity.

"Alex?" she wandered up the stairs and manoeuvred herself around the suitcases at the top of the stairs. "What's all this mess?"

He came bounding out of the bedroom, grinning from ear to ear. "I got my bonus, I have booked a treat for us." He kissed her on the top of his head. "Actually, I'm really excited, I hope you like it." He paused, kissed her on the mouth with a bit more enthusiasm than she was expecting and added, "Well, I might be terrified that you'll hate it, but I'm keeping my fingers crossed!"

"What have you booked?" she raised her eyebrows but excited nonetheless.

"I can't tell you, it's a surprise, but you need to pack – now!"

"Pack?"

"For a week!" And with that he left the bedroom and headed into the living room.

Lucy was left not knowing where to go or what to do. A break away for two sounded great. She'd moved in with him in the summer and they got on well together but they hadn't actually been away on holiday together yet. With no idea where they were going but excited nonetheless, she shouted, "Do I need a passport? Clothes for hot weather or cold?"

"We're staying in the UK." (Phew). "You'll need Christmas going out outfits, things for walking if we want to and just normal clothes otherwise," came the reply.

Within 15 minutes, Lucy had thrown her clothes on the bed, the excitement and the adrenaline erasing the end-of-term tiredness. A quick trip to the bathroom and she had everything needed for the suitcase. And no more than 30 minutes after walking through the door, unbelievably, she was ready to leave again. What a whirlwind this guy was. She was genuinely excited, felt festive in her Christmas jumper and was ready for the weather with her warmest coat, hat and scarf hanging on the banister.

Alex was just coming back from the flat below. "Jamie is going to have the milk when it is delivered on Monday and I've given him a few bits from the fridge." She looked her up and down and despite the layers she was wearing, she knew that he knew her stomach had just crumbled. She blushed. "You ready to go?"

"Yes!" she squealed, "Where are we going?"

"Train station. Taxi will be here in 15 minutes."

"Ooh, time for a brew?"

"Yes, but I've just given the milk to Jamie," he pointed at the floor and indicating the flat below.

Lucy laughed, Alex took a step towards her with a twinkle in his eye, "I know what there *is* time for!" He swept her off her feet and carried her into the bedroom. Her heart skittered as he pulled down her jeans and flipped her over onto the bed. Half on, half off the bed and giggling like a school girl, she heard him undo his belt and then she gasped as she felt his hands on the inside of her thighs. "Quick!" she laughed, "Taxi will be here…"

He took her, hard and fast and selfishly all for himself. Then leaning forward, his hands finding her breasts through the Christmas jumper and he whispered in her ear, "Your turn when we get there."

She loved it when he fucked her like that. The pleasure came from knowing that he wanted her that much and besides, the promise of later made her smile. The taxi beeped outside just as Lucy was rearranging her hair and checking her makeup in the mirror. Alex who was smoothing the sheets back into place, winked and smiled, "See, plenty of time!"

Once in the taxi, Alex relaxed. Getting Lucy out of Lancashire had been his main priority and now he could afford to take her away for Christmas. He couldn't bear the thought of another holiday involving another trip to the accident and emergency department with a beaten and bruised Lucy. No matter how much time the police dedicated to the investigation, no matter how they tried to convince Alex and Lucy it was 'just bad luck' and that there was no apparent link between the cases. Alex felt fobbed off and nothing, absolutely nothing was going to ruin their first Christmas together.

The train was on time and they found seats with a table at the end of the carriage. They had picked up coffee and cake for the journey and once they removed their coats and got comfy, Alex told Lucy where they were headed. "We're off to Edinburgh," he took a piece of paper from his jeans pocket. "This hotel, look. It's right next to the castle and we can explore the Christmas markets and do some late night shopping, or, we can just spend time cosied up in our suite."

"A suite?" she raised her eyebrows.

"Well," he winked, "Sort of, it's bigger than just one room. It has a sitting slash dining room area as well as a bedroom."

"So you can't keep me in bed for the whole week!"

"They've put a Christmas tree up for us," Alex continued, "And they'll do Christmas dinner. We can have either in the room or we can eat in the restaurant."

"I love it," Lucy was now googling the hotel on her phone and browsing the photos from guests. "It looks magical." She took both his hands in hers, "I can't wait to spend Christmas with you," she smiled.

They spent the journey chatting or relaxing in a companionable quiet, her head on his shoulder and his head on her head. She read her book, browsed Facebook, messaged Penny, *who was very excited* and he listened to music, smiled – a lot – and read his magazine. It had been dark when they embarked and it was even darker when they arrived in Edinburgh, found a taxi and arrived at the hotel.

"Room service for dinner?" Alex asked, "Or shall we go out-out?"

It was just after 8 p.m. and she was as tired as she was hungry. "Room service tonight please," she sat on the edge of the bed and unzipped her boots, rubbing the soles of her feet to get the circulation going again before taking a proper look around. It was spacious enough, she smiled as she wandered from the en-suite with double shower and the biggest bath she had ever seen (she knew how she would unwind tonight!) to the dining come sitting area with two high backed arm chairs, footstools, TV and dining table laid for two. There was an old open fire place where, instead of an actual open fire, there was a log burner and a stack of logs and a card (assumingly with instructions). How much had Alex spent on this!? She whistled on an exhale to show her approval and continued her wandering. She had never asked about his wages, she knew it was a decent, comfortable wage because he had refused to take any money from her towards the rent. The master bedroom and walk-in wardrobe was low lit with lamps and big shaggy rugs and, she blushed, the bed was enormous. Oh what fun they were going to have!

"You likey?" Alex remarked seeing the beaming smile on her face as he threw his now empty wash bag back into the suitcase, "Cosy isn't it?"

"Cosy?!" she squealed a little more girlish than she intended, but she wasn't quite able to contain the excitement. "It's out of this world!"

Alex grabbed her by the hands and moved her up against the wall, "I'd give you the world if I could afford and you mean the world to me." He kissed her and her groin began to ache with desire. She tried to put her arms around him but he found them and held them in his hands above her head, resting on the wall. They kissed with a fire and a passion that Lucy had never experienced with anyone else before and then Alex kissed her neck and her collar bone and Lucy let out a moan.

"We should eat," Alex said between kisses, "Before we get too carried away."

Lucy laughed, "I don't want to stop you, but I am starving."

Alex removed himself from Lucy and readjusted his trousers to accommodate his excitement. "We can enjoy this room for the next week."

They ordered food from the restaurant to be brought to the room which it was, and it was served up for them as if they were in the restaurant, housekeeping lit the log fire and the maître-de brought the wine. It took a moment for them to relax again after the unexpected bustle of other people in their space, but then they were gone and it was just the two of them again. They ate at the table, overlooking the city lights and the castle. Lucy felt so content, so safe and so, so happy. The red wine was warming up her cheeks and the log burner crackled behind them. This was pretty perfect. Pretty damned perfect.

The next morning, Lucy awoke to the low winter sun streaming in through the window, Alex, legs entwined with hers, was still asleep next to her. She lay on her side and looked at this perfect specimen of a man. How did she get so lucky? Well, life hadn't been the luckiest for her in recent months, but he was perfect. His dishevelled hair on the pillow brought back some red-wine-washed memories of the promised *your turn* and she blushed and closed her eyes to recall every perfect second of it.

He had joined her in the bath which had been a treat as he washed her hair and then held her in his strong arms. She had found herself so relaxed, and drunk, that she had told him all about her perfect-plan for the future. She had told him her dream was to be married (she cringed remembering her words) have two children, hopefully a boy and a girl and to be a successful teacher until retirement. She didn't need much to make her happy, just a man to love her and to spend the rest of his life devoted to her. Inhibitions removed by the bottle of wine, she hadn't even panicked that her words would scare him off and as he had replied (words also loosened by the wine) that he would be delighted to devote his life to her, she saw a new hope for the future.

For the first time since meeting, they had made love. Slow, tenderly, for each other's pleasure. Wordlessly asking for exactly what they wanted and it being granted. Hearts bursting and confident in each other's love they had climaxed together, rested and then carried on. It had been the most intense and yet the most intimate they had been with each other. Now, 'the morning after' Lucy wondered if he would still feel the same. She had bared her soul and she hoped that it had meant as much to him in the soberness of the morning. She opened her eyes again and saw him smiling at her.

"Morning gorgeous," he kissed her nose.

"Morning,"

"Good sleep?"

She sighed and smiled, "Very."

He rolled over on top of her his naked body against hers, "I should hope so. You were very energetic last night."

She lifted her hands to hide her blushing face.

"Don't hide," he was kissing her neck, working his way downwards, breasts, rib cage, stomach, pubic bone and then *there*. He paused, "It was the best night of my existence." He kissed her *there* again. She moaned and he took that to mean he could continue. "I promised you your turn, and I'm afraid I didn't keep my promise so here it is."

For the next twenty minutes or so, he kissed her and touched her, not taking a single piece of her for his own pleasure, focussing only on her. Bringing her to a cry-out climax again and again, until she clenched her legs together indicating that she could take no more of his mouth on her. She pulled him up to her face kissed him, then spread her legs and pushed herself up to meet him. With him inside her she allowed him his release thanking him once more for his love and attention.

"It's never been like this with anyone before you," he breathed into her ear. "You make me want to give so much more than I have. I love you Lucy Lawrence."

"I love you too," she smiled, kissed him and scooted out of bed for a shower.

Chapter 6

Fully unpacked into their accommodation and wrapped up with scarves and gloves, they headed out into the cold Scottish weather to warm themselves with mugs of Gluhwein and grilled sausage and cheese from one of the stalls. They chatted, laughed, browsed stalls and talked about their favourite parts of Christmas as children and as adults. They both agreed that Christmas Eve was special and that early get-ups to open presents on Christmas morning were essential, even if they had to go back to bed for a few hours.

"I bet you'd like that," Alex quipped, Lucy elbowed him slightly winding him, "No need for that level of aggression!" he joked.

"You are sailing dangerously close to the wind, young man!" Lucy laughed.

"Sorry Miss," came the reply followed by that school boy smile.

She humphed in mock annoyance, smiled and took his arm as they carried on walking.

The days leading up to Christmas were full of laughter and relaxed down-time. Alex had rarely seen Lucy so chilled and he had never been this happy. Previous relationships had become hard work and boring after a few months and yet, with Lucy, he could really see himself with her for, well, a long time – he wouldn't jinx it just yet.

They went to the ballet, ate good food and when Christmas eve came, they were both ready for an easy evening of Christmas films and room service in the hotel.

"Favourite Christmas film?" Lucy asked him.

"Well…" he started, only to be interrupted by her.

"Don't you dare say Die Hard," she laughed at the look of incredulity on his face.

"Okay, well, Home Alone. The first one, not the second. I mean, you wouldn't forget your kid twice would you?"

"Technically they didn't forget him in the second one, but yeah, a bit samey…"

"What about you?"

"The Holiday is my favourite,"

"Wait, I'm not allowed Die Hard, but you're allowed a film that is barely related to Christmas?" he mocked her.

"What? It is set at Christmas!"

"Nah, not having it. Choose another."

"Fine, let me think." Suddenly not a single Christmas film came to mind. She literally drew a blank. "I loved the dresses in White Christmas, as a child. I hate the Grinch's fingers," she shivered to show how much she disliked those long hairy fingers. "Arthur Christmas," she settled on.

"Good choice."

There was a knock at the door and their dinner came in on trolleys, followed by the maître-de. After dinner had been set up and the staff left, they continued their conversation.

"Favourite family tradition?"

"Opening a gift at midnight on Christmas eve," she smiled, "and stocking fillers before breakfast on Christmas morning. But that was when we were really young." She was smiling and the light from the fire made her look even more beautiful.

"Midnight?"

"Yeah, mum and dad used to do it, I overheard them once when I was about 12 and promised that when I grew up and got married, I would do the same." As soon as the words left her mouth, the shyness of sobriety reappeared and she quickly took a sip of the gin and tonic she had been nursing for the last hour.

Alex noticed how abruptly she had finished that sentence. He saw the fear that she was saying too much, giving too much of herself away and it made him love her even more – was that even possible? "For me, it was the family film on Christmas eve," he saw her instantly relax again as the normality of conversation flowed, "and the Queen's speech on Christmas Day."

"Oh good! I love watching the Queen's speech too."

"That's one thing sorted and set in stone for tomorrow then." He reached over the table and took her hand. "Please don't ever be shy and nervous to be yourself around me. I love you Lucy."

Her eyes met his and her heart missed several beats as she managed a smile. He squeezed her fingers and then went back to eating.

They watched A Muppets Christmas Carol and then the end of Elf on another channel. They drank cocktails and then decided to head down to the hotel bar to listen to the pianist. It was a good excuse to get dressed up. He wore a shirt and waistcoat with chinos and loafers and she wore her favourite black dress, sweeping her curls up onto the top of her head, she heard him wolf-whistle behind her then felt his hand on her backside.

"Down boy!" she joked, "We will never make it downstairs if you start on that now."

He laughed, "Am I not allowed to appreciate the utter beauty that is my girlfriend?"

Smiling as she put in her ear-rings, "I suppose if that is all you are doing, you may."

"Well, I am also undressing you," he started and Lucy attempted to interrupt him but he continued, "WITH MY EYES, only with my eyes, I'm allowed to do that?"

She cleared her throat, chuckled and carried on in the mirror. "I think I'm done." She turned around to pose for him, met his eye and caught his smile.

"Wow, you really are beautiful," he held out his hand.

"You don't look too bad yourself," she took his hand and together, they left the room.

Alex was watching the clock in the hotel lobby, 11:45 p.m. He had decided this evening that he was going to put his heart on the line. Lucy had bared her soul and yet kept getting flustered whenever her comments hinted at a longer, more permanent relationship. He knew that he had never spoken in that regards and she must have noticed too. Some things just need rectifying. He finished his whisky and iron-bru, a new one for him but recommended by the barman, and nice too.

"Hey," he whispered in her ear, "Want to head back to the room?"

She tilted her cocktail glass to see what was left, lifted it and drained it, "Yep, I think I am about ready for my beauty sleep."

He shot her a look that said, "You couldn't get more beautiful if you tried," and she laughed.

"Come on you loon, take me to bed," she was a little tipsy and a couple of lads at the bar raised their heads, gave Alex the thumbs up, grinned and went back to their drinks.

The lift chimed and they walked, hand in hand to their room, Alex swiping the key to gain entry. If he timed this right, Lucy would get her midnight wish. She went into the bathroom and began to remove her earrings and pull pins out of her hair, letting it fall across her shoulders.

Alex took a deep breath, 11.57 p.m. "Lucy?"

"Uh-hu?"

"Can you come here a second?"

He was standing at the window in their dining area looking out over the city. Twinkling lights met stars, it was really very pretty and perfect for what he wanted to say. He heard her come in behind him and saw her reflection in the glass. He turned to face her. "Lucy," he smiled at her. "Lucy, I am totally, absolutely, 100% head over heels in love with you. I just wanted you to know that."

"I know," she smiled back at him.

"I wanted to tell you that I loved you on our second date, but thought you might freak out, so I didn't." He stole a glance over her shoulder at the clock on the wall. 11.59 p.m.

"I might have," her shoulders gave her silent giggle away.

"So, I have saved it for now." He knelt down in front of her.

She gasped, "Alex?"

"Lucy Lawrence, I have loved you from the moment I spilt coffee all over you. And I know we've only been official for seven months, but when you know, you know. And I have fallen in love with you every day since then. I can't imagine my life without you." He put his hand into his shirt pocket and pulled out something small. The clock in the hallway stuck midnight and Alex smiled, perfect timing, "I want to spend the rest of my life with you, if you'll have me." He was looking into her eyes watching every possible emotion cross her face. "Will you marry me Lucy?" At the same time, the tears welled up in her eyes, she started to nod her head because she was speechless to say yes.

He placed the ring on her finger, kissed it and then brought her to him. Holding her tight, vowing to never let another thing happen to her as long as he lived. "I guess we just created a midnight tradition?" he asked, trying to avert her happy tears into laughter.

"Definitely," she smiled and kissed him. "Thank you for making this Christmas so perfect."

"It's not over yet!"

"You have more planned?"

"I have presents under the tree for you!"

She smiled and he held her in his arms for a little longer. The girl of his dreams had agreed to be his wife, he was the happiest man alive.

Waking up on Christmas day is exciting enough for most people, but waking up with a new, sparkly ring on your left ring finger, the guy you love in bed next to you *and* it's Christmas Day, well that was something else entirely. She rolled over to look at him. He really was so handsome. The bedclothes were wrapped around his waist and she studied the contours of his body, the dark hair on his chest, a day's worth of stubble on his chin. She loved it all. He was hers, and she was his. She sighed, as much as she wanted to open her presents, she didn't want to leave the yet. They'd had a late night, both opting to text their parents and closest friends with the good news. Alex had told his parents what he had intended to do and, even though they had only met her once, they knew that she made him happy. Lucy's mum knew too, Alex had been a gent there and her mum had even told him what size ring she was.

This might have been a last minute holiday, the proposal, was not however a last minute decision. It seemed that Alex had wanted to ask her for a while. His timing had been impeccable. Lucy had been starting to wonder if her open and honest conversations about her 'happy ever afters' were beginning to annoy him. Clearly not. Penny had called her the instant she had seen the picture message of her left hand and the ring, squealing in delight over the phone. They hadn't chatted long because Penny was out with her sister and it was very noisy. "I'm so happy for you," she had shouted down the phone line.

Lucy checked her Facebook. She had changed her status from 'in a relationship with' to 'engaged to' and she had a ton of notifications and messages of congratulations. She lay in bed being sure to acknowledge every well-wisher. About half an hour after her, Alex awoke. A smile on his face. "You did really say yes didn't you? I didn't dream it?"

"Say yes to what?" Lucy joked, holding up her hand and letting the daylight sparkle through the diamond solitaire.

"Come here you minx, kiss me,"

And she did, lovingly and completely.

Best Christmas ever. She felt a warm contentment as she smiled at Alex. So this was what love felt like. Knowing love was reciprocated made the feeling even more immense, deeper and much more tangible.

Chapter 7

2016

Rachel took one last look in the mirror. Her sleek black curls were super defined and her make-up was as good as it had ever been. Sophie had done her eyes and, well, WOW. Those wings. She turned her head left and then right, pushed her arms into her breasts to give her cleavage a boost and pouted in the mirror. Perfect. She hoped she would get some attention tonight, her sex life had been lacking a little recently. She held her phone up above her head, leant forward, tipped her head slightly right and puckered up her lips and took a picture. She repeated the process three or four times inspecting each photo for any minor flaw before deciding that the first one had in fact been the better of the bunch.

"Selfie?" she shouted into the bathroom.

"Yeah, I love this lip gloss, what do you think?" Sophie tottered into the room on her far-too-high heels, pouting.

"Beaut! You look amazing."

They posed together for several selfies, some serious, some funny, some vulgar. Same old, same old.

They were soon in the taxi on the way to their favourite Vodka Bar in the centre of Leeds, ID in their bags because being 19 years old and looking younger, they were usually asked for it, and they had plenty of money for a good night out.

"Don't forget, if Amy's brother is out, he's mine," Sophie tilted her head and caressed her breasts through her dress. "If I get even five minutes with him away from his mates, he won't be able to say no!" She smiled at Rachel, eyes sparkling. This girl had plans!

"So, if you suddenly disappear, I won't panic!"

"Exactly and I won't panic if I see *you* heading out with a tall dark and handsome stranger either!"

"Deal!"

"OMG we are going to have the BEST night out!"

They paid for the taxi and stepped out into the cold, December evening air. Let's get some alcohol in us, it's freezing. Sophie lit up a cigarette and took a deep drag, instantly relaxing. They stood in the queue outside REV's whilst Sophie finished smoking and chatted nonsense about Amy's brother and what *almost* happened last time. Rachel hoped that Sophie did get what she wanted, maybe then she would stop harping on about it. She also hoped that she'd meet someone attractive herself (or as attractive as a drunk man could be anyway) or tonight, she could be sat nursing a drink on her own, that would not be fun at all.

The girls drank, danced and chatted nonsense when Sophie nipped out for a smoke. For the first hour, there was absolutely no one decent to look at whatsoever. So they carried on drinking and slowly, better looking guys joined the crowd, or was that the alcohol taking effect?

"He's here!" Sophie elbowed Rachel in the gut, "Oh, sorry," she giggled seeing that Rachel had spilt her drink. She pointed very obviously at the group of guys who were hovering at the far end of the bar. "I'll be right back!" And with that Sophie, still as immaculate ever with her sleek blonde hair flowing down to her hips, tottered towards them. Eyeing up one of them with a look that needed no words, "Excuse me boys, I need a word with this one," and she took him by the hand. Surprisingly, Rachel thought he went rather willingly. Maybe everything Sophie had said *was* true then. Rachel laughed aloud and leaned over the bar to order herself another drink.

"You been abandoned?"

The deep, male voice was a lot closer to her ear than she could have expected, knowingly so by the fact that it wasn't shouting. Instead it was a breathy sound that startled but didn't scare her. She shot her best smile and fluttered her eyelashes half expecting to see some drunken try-hard working on his chat up lines. But no. Not a drunken boy at all. Short cropped hair, startling green eyes, clean shaven and biceps. Biceps that were defined by the tight white t-shirt as were the toned outline of his abs. She stopped herself mentally undressing him as the bartender came to serve her.

"Vodka Red Bull," she shouted over the noise.

"Make that two," he flourished a twenty pound note and then looking at her and shrugging, "You've been abandoned, my treat."

She wasn't about to turn down a free drink, even if he had been ugly as hell – which he wasn't, free vodka is free vodka. She glanced his way again, "Thanks," and then, "I need a name to thank you properly."

"Hmm?" he raised an eyebrow.

"Your name?" she shouted a little louder.

"What would be a sexy name for me?" he paid for the drinks and handed her one.

"Ha!" she took a big gulp of her drink. If he was playing hard to get, then so was she.

Sophie came up to the bar, flustered but smiling. "Oh my, how is my lipstick? Is my hair okay?"

Rachel laughed. "Not a hair out of place babes."

"Who's the hottie?" Sophie peered around her friend and nodded to the guy.

"Dunno," Rachel shrugged, "He won't tell me his name."

"Probably got a girlfriend."

" – Girlfriend or wife, He's far too hot to be single. And let's be fair, WAY out of my league!"

"Shut up!" Sophie slapped her friend playfully on the arm. "You are a catch!"

Getting impatient, Sophie shouted over the bar, "Is anybody serving tonight?"

The barman, popped his head up from the fridges below the counter-top. "Sorry love, what can I get you?"

"Five Jägerbombs please."

Minutes later, five Jägerbombs were lined up on the bar, Sophie waved her card and the barman held out the machine. Seconds later she was passing one of the shots to Rachel and beckoning to the guy who was back chatting to his mates.

"His name is Harry."

"What's your plan?"

"Few more drinks, then I think I get a shag tonight," she grinned, "You might too – if you play your cards right!"

Rachel chanced a glance back at the biceps man, "Maybe, maybe not."

Sophie kissed her on the cheek. Harry who had left his mates and re-joined her, was stood admiring her arse (who wouldn't) then he moved so close to her that he could have been fucking her over the bar. His face told a very good story of what he was after.

"Behave yourself, Harry!" Sophie squealed, but she loved the attention. She was definitely onto a winner tonight – so was Harry, Sophie was a trophy, wanted by every man, but quite specific in her own desires.

"Chat tomorrow!" Rachel smiled.

"Drink that in one," Sophie demanded handing her one of the shots - Rachel did. It hit the spot and she threw her head back laughing. "Have fun!"

Over the course of the next couple of hours, biceps guy had bought her a few drinks and the conversation had turned to filth – the usual, promises of the best night of her life. One that she wouldn't forget blah, blah. She'd heard it all before and not once had anyone delivered what they'd promised.

She laughed him off, "Whatever," and dragged him over to the dance floor.

They danced a bit, biceps guy could dance and was very enthusiastic at times, possibly on something a little stronger than alcohol, she couldn't be sure. That was not her sort of thing and she made a mental note to keep an eye for anything dodgy.

She noticed Sophie a couple of times on the dance floor; flaunting her gorgeous body, gaining plenty of attention as Harry's eyes warned off any other guy who took an interest; and then in the far corner of the club, making out. She wasn't sure at one point exactly where Harry's hands were but

Sophie was clearly getting some sort of pleasure by the look of her with her head thrown back, eyes closed, lips parted.

The night wore on with vodka in several forms and plenty of shots by the end. Sophie waved her goodbyes with a grin that said it all and Rachel checked her phone; just after three. She'd had fun, but needed food to soak up this vodka before getting herself a taxi home.

"I'm heading to the kebab house," Rachel shouted over the music to biceps guy. He had been dancing with her on and off throughout the night and when he was there she'd enjoyed the attention and when he wasn't, she'd been drunk enough to enjoy the dance floor nonetheless. She had always been confident in this place, probably because she had been here many, many times. Most Friday nights since she looked old enough to escape the ID check, about 16 years old?

He nodded and held up his drink indicating that he was almost done, "I'll catch you up."

She was a little miffed that he was in no rush to join her and resolved to get food, not hang around waiting for him and get a taxi home. But as she was paying for her food, she caught sight of him on his phone just outside the door. He looked cross. Maybe he did have a girlfriend and she was giving him hell for being out late. She walked past him and sat on the wall as he finished his call.

"So, you inviting me back to yours?" he raised an eyebrow.

"Because your girlfriend is at your place?"

"Is that a problem?" he cocked his head.

An honest guy, that was unexpected. Rachel smiled, "So, if I don't get to know your name – presumably because you don't want some young girl hunting for you on Facebook and disturbing your life -" he smirked and half nodded, "What can I call you?"

"Tom, you can call me Tom."

"Okay, then Tom," she checked her phone, "That's my taxi." She stood up and walked over to the white Focus that had just pulled up. He held back a seconds to admire her long slender legs then stood up to catch the small of her back on, showing some chivalry at least.

Back at hers, Rachel was glad she'd made the bed this morning. Tom was at least fifteen years older than her and she wanted to appear mature and not school girlish – unless that was his thing. She cringed at the thought.

He looked around her room and noted that she was obsessed with her looks, selfies stuck to the mirror along with lipstick kisses in various shades, about twenty dresses on hangers in the open wardrobe, none of them modest. Heels and bags, far too many to count and makeup, lots of it; in boxes, on display and strewn across the table top. There was an empty bottle of wine on the bedside table and a pack of condoms. Good, he thought. At least this was consensual and a pre-conceived ending to her night.

She spun around and started to undress. Unhooking her dress from behind her neck, she let the dress fall forward to reveal the pertest tits he had ever clapped eyes on. She wriggled her hips confidently letting it fall to the floor an confidently stepping of it and walked towards him in only a pair of black lacy panties and her heals. He was impressed with her confidence. It was quite clear what she wanted, this wouldn't require much effort. In one movement, he removed his t-shirt and enjoyed the movement of her eyes as she looked over his toned body. He picked her up and carried her to the bed dropping her roughly so that he could remove his jeans. None of this was in the plan he'd made for tonight, but it was so clearly on offer and damn it, he found her attractive in a slutty way. Plus she had condoms – she wanted this too.

He went straight for her stomach with his teeth, grazing them along her tanned skin. She had goose bumps. "You look good enough to eat," he breathed. He grabbed a condom from the side of her bed and sheathed himself. He didn't have time or energy for more foreplay than that. He pulled her panties to the side and spat onto his finger rubbing them roughly between her legs. He stepped closer and took her. More harshly than she was used to he assumed as her eyes widened. He didn't care. She wouldn't remember this by tomorrow. She wouldn't even be here anymore. He lifted her legs above his torso and onto his shoulders, she had closed her eyes and was trying to find some. This was obviously not how she usually had her men. He didn't care. He grabbed her hips and thrust deeper and harder. His eyes on her face. She wasn't enjoying it one bit, her face was tensed and he saw her regret. He came with a grunt and pulled out of her. She didn't open her eyes.

"You can leave now," she almost cried.

"Not quite yet."

Her eyes flickered open as he was taking something from his jeans pocket, putting it in his mouth. He sat on the bed next to her and forced his lips onto hers, sticking his tongue and whatever it was into her mouth. Eyes wide now, she realised too late what had happened. Drugs. The room went hazy, her body relaxed. Her thoughts were wandering and she tried to speak but couldn't. The room span and her eyes closed.

Chapter 8

2010

There is a reason why sleep deprivation is used as a form of torture and if it wasn't for the love Megan felt for the small boy bawling his eyes out, she would have closed the door and gone back to bed. Tired as she was, she paced back and forth at the foot of her bed. This was not what she had expected from motherhood, awake every hour for feeds, her barely getting back to sleep in between, it was the hardest thing she had ever done. Yet, when she looked at him, the frustration melted away and she would do anything for him.

Still dark outside, she worked out that it was somewhere between 3 a.m. and 5 a.m., based on the last wakeup and the distinct lack of birdsong in the garden. She shivered, not through cold, but through the adrenaline kicking in once again. She might, if she was lucky, get another hour's sleep if he would stay asleep long enough. She paced the end of the bed for another five minutes just to make sure he was well and truly asleep, gently placed him in the small crib at the side of her bed and fell, dressing gown still on, into her bed.

They had waited a long time for their bundle of joy. Years of trying, finding out that they wouldn't be able to conceive naturally and then two rounds of IVF. The first failed attempt had broken her heart and she wasn't sure she could go through the hope and the let down again. But Michael wanted so desperately to have a child that she gave it one more shot. It had worked and although nothing had ever hinted at any complication, she had been on edge the entire pregnancy, waiting for something bad to happen.

She didn't know what she had done to deserve this beautiful boy but some days it felt as if it would all be whipped away from her in an instant. But no, a full 41 weeks of pregnancy had seen them welcome their beautiful boy into the world. Thomas Michael Simpson had been born on July 19th 2010 weighing 8 lb 1 oz. and screaming to make sure the entire world was aware of his arrival.

Since then, the love she felt had only grown. Her world revolved around the small bundle and if anyone else wanted to hold him, it was allowed, but only fleetingly. She needed him close to her. He was a part of her and a mother's love, after years of waiting, was not one to be questioned. She would spend the days gazing at the sleeping child when she should have been getting some rest and the nights, begging for him to sleep so that she could too.

Megan hadn't returned to work when Thomas was born, instead she had made the decision to stay at home. This meant that she had been able to spend every minute of his little life by his side. She watched him learn to roll and crawl, she taught him to feed himself; making a mess at first but soon learning to find his mouth. She heard his first words and watched him take his first steps. The thought of being at work to pay someone else to care for him was absurd. No mother should have to be a part from her child for any length of time. In fact, she resolved that paid maternity leave was nowhere near long enough and that it should be at least double, on a full wage! It certainly wasn't cheap to keep a baby fed, warm and entertained.

His first birthday came and went, as did his second. They were on holiday in Wales for his third and had a big party with all his friends for his fourth. Life was good and the happy little four-year-old started school. He came home from school every day with a new tale to tell and she couldn't have been more proud.

The years flew by and people would tell her, with the age-old cliché that, 'He'll grow up so fast, make the most of it,' and Megan would laugh it off with, "He'll be my baby forever." He really would be, at no point in his life would he not be her blessing, her answered prayer, her gift from God. This was her one chance to be a mum and she would be damned sure that she gave it her best shot.

By the age of five, he was the spitting image of his daddy and people would comment that he would break hearts when he was older. He had jet black hair and green eyes, freckles dotted over the bridge of his nose and onto his cheeks. When he smiled there was a dimple on the left and his nose would wrinkle, just like his dad.

Megan's mum passed away just before Thomas started school and her dad shortly afterwards. She began to feel the anxieties from her pregnancy return. The fear of losing loved ones kept her awake at night and she held Thomas a little closer and stayed a few minutes longer cuddling him to sleep at night. Breathing in the scent of him calmed her nerves, grounded her and brought her back to the realisation that she was already luckier than she ever could have imagined.

"I think I need a job," she announced to Michael one night. The winter nights were drawing in and Christmas was looming. "It would help with Christmas."

"It's completely up to you," he put his arm around her and pulled her close. "We manage." He kissed the top of her head.

"Yeah, but Thomas is in school most of the day and I end up doing nothing except watching TV, to be honest I'm bored," she laughed.

"Well I never thought I would hear you say that." He put his newspaper down, "What would you do?"

"Anything, as long as I can do it while Thomas is in school."

"So a ten 'til two sort of thing?" he suggested.

"Yeah, that would work. And not too far away, I could get the bus or walk."

"We'll have a look tomorrow, shall we?"

"Sounds like a plan," she smiled and snuggled into the crook of his arm to watch TV.

"Sounds like a plan," he agreed.

Just three weeks later, Megan was dropping Thomas off at school and heading on to work. She had managed to get a part time job in customer services about a mile from home. It was a basic wage but the staff were friendly and, because it was a 24/7 customer service line, she was able to work flexibly in the school holidays to make sure there was always someone to look after Thomas. It had been a great find, perfect for her in so many ways.

Two weeks after she started, she received her first wage and it felt good to be able to treat her little family to a chippy tea without worrying about the bills. The following months she treated herself to a new coat, having been wearing the same coat since before Thomas was born, she felt like a new woman in it. Every month, she was able to treat herself and her family and she felt like she could really thank Michael for everything he had done for her over the past four and a bit years.

For the first time in quite a few years she saw that her life as a whole, not just being a mum, was good. Since giving birth, she had felt the weight of the world on her shoulders and often saw the negativity and not the positives in everything around her. Now, she really did have everything she needed and she appreciated every day's new adventure. Even the hard times: walking to work in the rain, Thomas having a tantrum at bath time, Michael falling asleep on the sofa and burning the dinner in the oven, were more bearable with her new positive outlook on life. She smiled more and when she smiled, the world seemed to smile back at her. As her wages started to build up in her bank, she wondered if she would even be able to treat Michael and Thomas to a holiday in the summer, just to say thank you and to show them how much she loved them both.

Chapter 9

2018

Returning to work after the Christmas holidays, Lucy was loving the attention. Instead of returning to school with more bruises and a police report, she had returned smiling and showing off a sparkling solitaire on the ring finger of her left hand. She regaled the story to anyone who asked, she was blissfully happy.

The weeks flew by. Her mum wanted to know if it was a long engagement or if they would be setting a date any time soon. Lucy grinned whenever she called – which was alarmingly often compared to usual – because she knew her mum wanted to take her one and only daughter wedding dress shopping. So when Lucy and Alex actively began looking at wedding venues and contacting them for availability, Lucy was thrilled to tell her mum that they were looking for dates within the year.

"This is the happiest day of my life!" her mum had squealed in excitement.

"No mum, that's my line. You don't get to steal it from me!" They had both laughed and Lucy agreed that once the colour scheme was decided, the flowers and table decorations could be her mum's 'baby' and of course her mum wanted to pay for the dress.

By the end of the February half term, they had chosen their venue and the date for their wedding. Having both had the week off, they'd spent every day together walking, taking the train for days out, daytime drinking and generally enjoying the little things in life. They paid their deposit on the Friday and toasted the date that they would officially become husband and wife, 20th October 2018, with a champagne breakfast on the final Sunday of the holidays.

Life was perfect, the struggles of the previous year were almost a distant memory and Lucy was finally able to get out and about with her old level of confidence again. Although she had to admit, she didn't do much alone anymore. In the working week, Penny was always checking in on her and at the weekends, she and Alex would do things together. But that was how it was meant to be, wasn't it? Being looked out for by those who love you? Lucy smiled. They both loved her and she couldn't imagine her life without either of them. Thankfully she never would.

"Penny?" Lucy called as she walked into the neighbouring classroom one Monday morning in March.

"I'm in the cupboard," was the reply followed by the sound of boxes being put on shelves and the huffing and puffing of a rather dusty Penny as she emerged. "We have to sort those boxes of books out. There are far, far too many that we don't use anymore."

Lucy laughed, "You should have shouted me to help."

"I didn't realise what I was getting myself in to back there! Anyway, what's up?"

"I wanted to ask you something. Something important."

"Oh yeah? Need wedding advice from the only woman in school who is single and carefree?" she rolled her eyes and Lucy laughed.

"Kind of."

"Oh, go on then, shoot."

"I need someone I love, who is a size 14 dress, size 6 shoe, tanned with long blonde hair who looks good in the colour olive to be my bridesmaid…"

Penny's face showed thoughtfulness as she worked her way through the requirements before realising what Lucy was asking. Then, she beamed and laughed. "You would do that to me on a Monday morning, wouldn't you?"

"Well? Will you be my bridesmaid?" she cocked her head and smiled at Penny, "I would ask you to be my maid of honour… but… well –"

"I know, I know. I'm not married. I can't help it that I'm picky," she laughed.

"So, is that a yes?"

"Of course it's a yes Lucy. I would be honoured." Penny threw her arms around Lucy and her eyes prickled with the threat of tears.

"I will make sure that Alex invites plenty of good looking guys for you to choose from!"

"Muchly appreciated," Penny laughed.

The months flew by as the wedding planning and preparations unfolded, it was soon May. Alex's cute friend Harvey was the best man (Lucy planned to introduce him to Penny), his uncle was going to do the photographs. A local florist known to Lucy's mum was doing the flowers, and one of the teaching assistants at school was doing the cake for them. Today however, was the most exciting day to date. Lucy and her mum were dress shopping.

They started the morning with some champagne at the flat and then caught a taxi into town. The wedding boutique looked small from the outside but was three stories high and had the best reputation from brides for finding their perfect dress.

The owner of the shop was their host today. Thankfully she was a patient woman because Lucy had no idea what style, length or colour she wanted. By lunch time that, at least, was narrowed down to three-quarter length and white.

"How is it going?" Alex was asking her over the phone.

"I am exhausted! I've never gotten dressed and undressed so many times in my entire life!"

"But you've found one you love?"

"Not yet!" Lucy must have sounded exasperated because her mum had moved over to pat her gently on the knee.

"You will. And you will look amazing."

"I hope so," she sighed. "They're coming back with more dresses, I must be the most difficult bride-to-be they've ever had!"

"I bet that's not true. Every bride deserves to try on every dress until they find the perfect one!" he comforted her.

The staff were now wheeling in a rail with more dresses in the newly specified length and colour, "Got to go, more dresses to try on! Love you."

"Love you more."

Lucy was ushered into the changing room once more, four dresses later and Lucy emerged in the dress she was confident was 'the one.' She walked out to her mum sitting on the chair and by the look on her mum's face, Lucy knew she was right.

"It's perfect Lucy," she was up and fussing now. Lucy thought she might have seen a tear in her eye. "Just perfect," she smiled and turned to dab her eyes. "Now we need to think about a veil and shoes."

"Not today mum, I'm knackered." Lucy then panicked and turned to the owner. "Can I come back to choose the veil? I don't think I have the energy for more today."

The answer was yes, of course she could and when Lucy was finally back in her jeans and t-shirt, her mum took a photo of her with the 'I said yes to the dress' flag which she sent to Alex and Penny and then posted to Facebook. Four and a half hours after they had arrived, they left the shop Lucy smiling and although she was tired, she was more excited than she had been in quite a while. The dress was staying at the shop for all her fittings and she could choose shoes and a veil next time she came. She was glad to see the sky again and she turned her face skywards and smiled. Today was a good day.

"Let's get us something to eat," mum suggested pointing towards the town centre. "The Royal Oak? Or Frankie's?"

"You choose," Lucy liked both so left the decision in her mum's hands.

"Frankie's it is then."

Lucy nodded and they headed around the corner towards the quaint cafe. She was tired and hungry and wanted to sit down and process the morning.

"I need coffee," she joked.

Just as she was about to cross the road, Lucy was aware of a presence close behind her. She turned and was about to ask the person to respect her personal space when she met his eyes. A scream caught in her throat as *that man* grabbed her wrist and twisted her arm fast and hard that she had no choice but to follow it to the ground. She winced as a pain shot up her arm. He released her arm which fell with the sudden lack of support, to the ground. "Ouch," she thought

"Lucy?" her mum cried out but was quickly silenced by what she saw. "What? No!"

Lucy heard her mum scream before she felt a heavy stamp to her back. She hit her head on the pavement and was sure she felt her nose break with the impact. Instinct told her to try and crawl away, but as she tried, she felt her hair being yanked and saw his foot come at her face with such force that she had no time to scream.

Then he was crouching down and his face was so close to hers that she could smell his stale breath. Her ears were ringing. His mouth was moving and he was speaking to her. But the pain surged through her and she closed her eyes.

And with that he was gone.

Lucy was aware of her mum's screams and sobs as she sat on the ground to tend to her daughter. She tried to tell her that she was okay, but she couldn't and she wasn't. She closed her eyes and the pain flooded through her central-nervous system. It hurt to breath, it hurt to think; everything hurt. She was sure that every bone in the right side of her face was broken and she worried that her mum might die of shock.

The world was moving in slow motion as Lucy became aware of people around her but she couldn't focus on anything. The pain was too much, she would be happy to die right there, just to get away from the pain. Her eyes flickered shut.

Lucy was vaguely aware of the paramedics. Police. People. They put her in a neck brace, rolled her and transferred her onto a stretcher and into the waiting ambulance. Her mother wanted to stay with her but was told that another ambulance was on its way for her. She sat with the first responder, wrapped in a foil blanket, shivering from the fright and the shock of witnessing such a brutal and violent attack on her daughter and being too old and useless to do anything to stop it from happening.

Onlookers whispered, huddled in small groups around the scene discussing what they knew and what they had seen. Some spoke to the police and made statements, but no one really knew what had happened. The only person who had seen it all was the mother and right now she was being treated for shock and passing Alex's number onto a police officer.

Arriving at the hospital, Alex used the emergency medical staff entrance and asked the closest paramedic where he would find his fiancé, the woman who has been violently attacked in town. He hated this place. It brought back all the memories of previous visits and reminded him of the times he had been unable to protect Lucy from the man who seemed to have it in for her. Who would want to hurt Lucy?

She was the gentlest, kindest and most caring girl he had ever met. She wouldn't do anything to hurt anyone, in fact she would do whatever she could to help anyone who needed it.

He was shown the bay where nurses stood surrounding the trolley, making notes and setting up machines. No matter how many times, he had seen her being treated for her injuries, it still broke his heart. He longed to hold her hand and reassure her, but she was clearly out of it and being well looked after. He caught the attention of one of the nurses, explained who he was and asked what was going to happen now.

"She's going to theatre in the next available slot," the nurse looked at his watch, "in about 30 minutes and the doctor will look at her cheek bone and see what can be done. Without an x-ray, we can't be sure – but it's possibly shattered from the blow and she needs will need an MRI on her spine to check the damage there.

"Where is her mother?"

"Sorry?"

"Her mother had a paramedic call me, she was also being put in an ambulance?"

"Oh okay, let me check."

Alex lifted his head as a gush of air blew through the double doors and he saw Maggie being brought in through the doors in a wheelchair. He felt a rush of love for the dishevelled woman. She hadn't been sure of him when Lucy had first introduced him to her. Too focussed on his studies, would soon lose interest – in other words she thought he was a geek! Thankfully he had proved her wrong. Her face was flushed, her cheeks wet and her eyes wide and bloodshot.

"Oh Alex," she cried when she saw him.

"Maggie," he rushed to her side. "What happened?"

"He came out of nowhere, had her on the ground kicking the shit out of her for absolutely no reason," the tears started to fall again. "There was nothing I could do."

He crouched down and put his arm around her trembling shoulders. The warmth of his touch helped to calm her nerves and it wasn't long before she stopped trembling but the tears that had started, continued to roll down her face.

"The police," she continued, "They were in the ambulance with me, waiting to ask me more questions after I've been seen by the doctor."

"Don't worry about that just now," he lovingly shushed her cries, "Let's get you sorted and find out what is happening with Lucy."

At the mention of her daughter's name, she started to look around the small department, "Where is she?"

He pointed to the end bay and the crowd of nurses and doctors. They're taking her straight into theatre." His face tensed up. "Her face – "

"I saw it," Maggie shook her head. "What a mess."

"Okay, Mrs Lawrence?" a nurse walked over to the wheelchair. Maggie nodded and squeezed Alex's hand before letting go. "Let's make sure you're okay, shall we?"

Alex let her go with the nurse as he waited, leaning against the wall. His heart was breaking but there was nothing he could do but wait for the doctors to do what they could for Lucy.

Chapter 10

"You did what?" the blonde haired woman screamed.

The man shrugged and pushed past her to get to the fridge and took a can of beer from it. He pulled the tab and breathed out. "She deserved it." He took a slug of his beer and headed towards the sofa.

The room was small and the curtains stopped most of the light from coming through. He kicked off his shoes, he sat down and put his feet up.

"What?" the blonde haired woman had followed him in and was staring at him with rage.

"SHE deserved it," he repeated, spitting the word 'she' with hatred.

"You can't just walk around beating the crap out of people!" she was exasperated. "If they catch you," she paused, taking a moment to calm the fear and anxiety that was rising in her chest, "What will I do then?"

He didn't reply.

She slumped down into the armchair in the corner. "Did you do the shopping?"

He nodded towards the bag by the kitchen door. She smiled outwardly, "Thank you." What would she do without him? She relied on him for everything now that she was housebound. He did her shopping, went to the bank for her, he also did all the small things that she would no longer do like putting out the bins, fetching parcels from the neighbour's house because she couldn't answer the front door to the postman.

They had been together for eighteen years, married for fourteen. Life hadn't always like this. They had been happy. So happy. The last year had taken its toll on both of them, it had aged them, made them bitter and selfish. Their love had evolved from what it had been in the beginning. She was no longer carefree, he was no longer calm and collected.

As they sat in the darkness, he looked over at her. Her forehead was furrowed where there were once smile lines and her hair was wiry and dry where it used to be glossy. He could still see the old her, in her eyes. Sometimes, when she was deep in thought, far away from the cares of this life, he saw the sparkle in them that he had fallen in love with. His heart ached for her. If he could have one thing in life gifted to him, it would be her happiness. The pain and anxiety of the last eleven months had caused their relationship to change so dramatically that they had almost broken up, thankfully he'd had the strength to fight for their relationship. They still loved each other, more deeply than either would let on, but he hated what she had become and she despised his angry outbursts.

"Well, you're going to have to stay in the house for a few days now." The anxiety started to rise in her chest, the tightening, then the rapid heartbeat. She breathed in slowly and then exhaled. "I can't risk you being caught." She felt the imminent panic attack and by the way he moved in the chair opposite, she knew that he felt it too. "The police will be all over town *again*," she cursed his stupidity under her breath, closed her eyes and counted backwards from ten. She had to keep him safe, like he had kept her safe when she had been at her lowest; when she had done nothing but cry for days on end. He had sat with her, fed her, washed her, and when her world had been as black as the night, he had still loved her. She loved him too. Despite everything. The connection, the fear of losing him, the need to protect him was still there.

They sat in silence. Her regulating her breathing, him drinking. Both of them worrying about how life might change. How it could all be ripped apart at the seams if the police came knocking at their front door. Once again, because of his stupid, irrational actions, they would have to go on lockdown, again.

He drained his can, stood up, closed the curtains and headed to the kitchen to put the shopping away. She didn't open her eyes but he could see the fear etched into the worry lines of her brow. He listened to her breathing, meditating and controlling her anxieties. She had come a long way this year. He was so proud of her. She had overcome so much.

He had too but that had almost been overlooked. When she had been so poorly, all the attention had been on her. All the help, support, medical intervention, counselling. He'd had to be strong, for her. Which in turn had meant locking away his own pain and anger. He knew that what he had done today was wrong. But seeing that mop of black curls had brought it all back. The pain had seared through his heart like a white hot poker. It made him barely human, unfeeling, ruthless. He had not been able to control himself.

Her distress had made him feel even worse. He held her world together. If anything happened to him, she would not survive it. His love for her, the fear he had surrounding her sat like a ball of heat inside his chest, threatening to choke him. He leant on the kitchen counter, took a deep breath and exhaled slowly. He had learnt that from her. Listening to how *she* breathed when her anxiety started to take control. It worked. He stood up again and started to put the shopping away. He wiped the kitchen sides and then looked out at the over grown and unloved garden. It hadn't been touched in a year. The neighbours used to complain but it was futile. The long grass and overgrown shrubs protected his wife from what was out there.

He picked up the photo frame on the windowsill. Their wedding day. He remembered it vividly. The sun had shone favourably on them, the clear blue, cloudless sky, sun radiating in every photo taken that day. There had been laughter and happiness. There had been love. There had been so much love shared between their family and friends. She had danced, like no one was watching. She had kissed him without inhibitions. She had smiled until her cheeks hurt. He smiled fondly at the memories. He couldn't recall the last real smile he had seen on her face. Nor could he recall the last time that she had sang along to the radio or danced. She was a broken woman. But God, she was HIS broken woman and there was nothing that he wouldn't do for her.

A tear appeared unexpectedly and rolled down his cheek. The love he felt for this woman would heal her – if she let him. If Megan would just let him love her like she used to. They could be happy again, a different sort of happy, but still happier than, than *this*. He wiped away the tear.

Michael coughed to clear his throat and the lump that was threatening to give way to his emotions and began to put the pots from the drainer away. Where was life headed for them? He did not know. He couldn't see past the end of the day. Every day, he just fumbled in the darkness. And with his actions today, he had brought another dark cloud down on them.

Chapter 11

Rachel woke up with a thumping headache and the feeling that her blood still contained far too much alcohol. She reached for her phone to see what time it was. Wait, where was her bedside table? She attempted to sit up but the room started to spin. Maybe she had gone back to someone's house last night? She couldn't recall. But hey, who cared, she was obviously still drunk and so she closed her eyes again, sleep was easy.

She awoke again a few hours later, not feeling particularly better but she should really be making her way home. She needed a shower, the smell of cigarette smoke lingered in her curls and urgh, she touched her face, she's slept in her makeup – gross, she'd definitely be cleansing her skin today. Nobody wants skin break outs from sleeping in full makeup. She rubbed her eyes to help wake herself up and opening her eyes she surveyed the room around her. Dismal. There was no other word for it. She'd really lowered her standards this time. Mattress on the floor, blankets tucked over a rail at the windows, a rug over bare floorboards. Maybe she would need an STI test too, just in case the guy was as grim as this place. She stood up and wandered around the room carefully picking up her belongings. Maybe she could sneak out and get a taxi home without being seen. But, where was her phone? She checked under the mattress, in her jacket pocket, in her bag. Shit. That phone had cost her a fortune. She'd need to get a block put on that. Sophie would kill her if she didn't text an update on her night.

What actually had happened last night? She had absolutely no idea, she couldn't even remember leaving the club. She looked out of the window, she was in a high rise flat, probably three floors up. Nothing she saw was recognisable. She hated it when this happened - thankfully it didn't happen often. Usually she'd get laid by nice guys, in nice apartments. This place was a shit hole, she guessed she could say it was the price you pay when you don't want to settle into a relationship, want good nights out to drink and have sex with random strangers. It was her choice and she loved her life – well, maybe not this aspect, but the rest was pretty great.

She threw her coat around her shoulders and, choosing to leave her heels off until she got down the stairs, she headed for the door. She turned the handle as quietly as she could. Nothing. She tried again. Locked? Panic rose in her chest. Why the hell was the door locked?

"Hey!" she shouted. "Let me out!"

She waited for a reply. Nothing. She shouted again.

"NOT funny! Let me out this instant."

Still no answer. Who the hell would lock their one night stand in a room? She went to the window and tried to open it so she could lean out and get a better look but it was locked as well. She looked again at the view from the window; tall flats surrounding the one she was in. She tried to work out where she was, this didn't look like any part of Leeds she'd been to before.

She went back to the door and started to bang on it with her fists, she hated to admit it, but she was actually starting to feel a little scared now. She'd never been scared before. Without her phone, she felt uneasy and without anything to tell the time on, she had no concept of time and so she continued to bang and scream at the door until her hands hurt and she had no energy left. Screaming had left her throat sore and she needed a drink. Helpless, she headed back to the mattress on the floor and sat on it. What the hell had she done this time?

It was getting darker outside now, she could only guess at the time. Definitely evening and she was starving hungry. There was a noise somewhere, above her? Next to her? She wasn't sure, but someone was about and so she took the opportunity to let whoever it was know that she wasn't happy with being imprisoned in this shit-hole.

"Hey! Scumbag, let me out of this place. How dare you lock me in this scabby excuse for a home." She banged her fists on the door again, not as loud, the skin was still raw from before.

Footsteps! Finally. She picked up her belongings ready to get out as soon as the door opened. She heard a key in the lock and mustered all the strength she had left as the door started to swing inwards, making her face look as fierce as she felt.

"Where do you think you are going?" a man in jeans and a shirt asked, she didn't recognise him.

"Home!" she started to barge past him but he blocked her path.

"I don't think you are," he pushed her roughly into the room and closed the door. "You make too much noise."

"I want the hell out of this place," she demanded.

"That's not going to happen gorgeous."

"You don't get to call me that. You scumbag."

He laughed in her face. "Scumbag?" he slapped her around the face with the back of his hand. "Scumbag? You're a slut!" he walked toward her so suddenly that she stepped backwards to get out of the way. Instead, she tripped and landed on the mattress, the wind knocked out of her. He kept on coming until he was pinning her down underneath him. She screamed and he laughed in her face, "You're a slut. And you're mine." Straddling her stomach, he reached into his pocket and took something out of a small box. He roughly grabbed her face, his thumb on one cheek and the rest of his fingers on the other cheek and squeezed so that her lips parted. He forced something into her mouth and then blew in her face so that she had to take a breath in and then he squeezed her lips closed so that she couldn't spit out. "Now shut up."

Her world fell into darkness.

She was awoken at some point in the night by a girl of a similar age. "Here, I have food for you." The girl was stroking her face and smiling.

"I'm tired," Rachel sighed.

"You need to eat. Come on, it's pizza," she wafted a slice under Rachel's nose and smiled when that gained a response.

Rachel sat up slowly. The room was lit by a lamp in the corner and there were more mattresses in here now. Or was this another room? "Where am I?"

"It doesn't matter." The girl looked away, "You don't need to know that."

"What is this place?"

"You don't want to know. Eat up, you must be starving," she passed a slice of pizza over the mattress and this time Rachel took it. She was hungry. She couldn't remember the last time she'd eaten.

"How long have I been here?"

"Three days." The look on Rachel's face prompted her to say more. "You were pretty out of it until today."

"Out of it?"

"Sleeping a lot." The girl wasn't making eye contact. "Look, just eat, we can talk afterwards."

Rachel ate. The pizza was good and she was handed a bottle of water. She drank.

"I need to get home," her eyes were pleading with the girl. "I need to get out of here."

There was no response. The girl just picked at her pizza.

"Did you hear me? I need to get out? How do I get out?"

"You don't," she paused, opened her mouth as if she was about to say something else but changed her mind and ate some more pizza instead. "Just accept it, don't ask questions, do as you're told and you'll be okay. I'm Jen, by the way."

"I'm -"

"Rachel, I know."

The days passed. Rachel cried, slept, woke, cried and ate whenever food was offered, which wasn't often. But then she wasn't interested much in food. She wanted to go home. She wanted to wash this place off her. She heard men's voices somewhere close by and tried to work out what they were saying. But they were either too far away or not speaking English and she couldn't work out what was being said.

She managed to wash in the sink in the small bathroom – there was a toilet, a sink and a bucket. The toilet didn't flush well so the bucket had to be used from time to time.

Whenever she kicked off, which was quite a bit in the first few weeks, she was put in her place with either a fist or a foot and then drugged. Jen, who in Rachel's eyes had already given up, tried to talk her down before that happened, but Rachel had no intention of giving up without a fight. She was drugged whenever she fought, which was often. It was the only time she felt any peace.

Chapter 12

Maggie was sat with a now cold coffee between her hands and Alex was pacing the waiting room. A family liaison officer had been assigned and she was sitting next to Maggie, company if nothing else, but also there to answer any questions they may need to ask. Lucy had been in surgery for 6 hours now and they had heard nothing. It was 10 p.m. when Alex went to the nurse's station, "Can we get an update on Lucy Lawrence please?"

The nurse looked over the top of her glasses and recognising Alex from the waiting room, nodded and walked to the nurse station at the far end of the corridor. He could see her talking to another nurse who then made a phone call. They were leaning towards each other, discussing Lucy? Or having a catch up? Alex knew he was being impatient and grumpy – with good reason of course, but still, he wanted answers. They could talk on their break, surely?

His phone vibrated in his back pocket, his mum.

How is she?

No one is telling us anything.

They won't want to tell you anything until they are certain about it.

I want to know if she's okay!

She will be! She's a tough cookie.

She shouldn't have to be!

The nurse was walking back towards Alex now. He put his pocket away and beckoned to Maggie to come and join him.

"She's out of theatre."

They both audibly sighed, "The surgeon will be out to talk with you shortly."

"Thank you," Maggie smiled weakly and headed back to her seat, the cold cup of coffee still in her hand. Alex followed suit and say back down.

A police officer poked her head around the door frame, nodded at the family liaison officer and Alex and then entered.

"We have some CCTV of your fiancés attack."

"Can you identify him?" Maggie looked up and asked, "From the footage?"

"Not yet."

Alex stood up, the balls of his palms in his pressing into eye sockets in frustration. This was the second time the

CCTV footage had been a waste of time. He clenched and unclenched his fists.

"But using that footage," the officer continued, "We have been able to find the same male in a series of footage from other CCTV cameras operating in the area. We will get him."

"I want to ask him why." Maggie spoke quietly. Lucy was certainly this woman's daughter, Alex thought. Calm and collected. No rage, No anger. Just the need for answers to make sense of it all.

"I want to do more than ask him why!" Alex spoke through a tense jaw.

"Oh, he will get what he deserves, and in front of a judge too," the officer assured. "This is the third time?" she looked at Alex.

"Yes."

"Your fiancé managed to tell the officers at the scene that this was the same man as the previous attack." The police thought that it very likely that the first attack had been him as well. The officer's radio started transmitting and she left the room to reply. Alex couldn't hear what was being said.

He started pacing the room again. Pulling his hands through his hair clearly agitated.

It wasn't long before the door at the far end of the corridor opened and Alex heard the distinct squeak of shoes on vinyl coming towards them. Maggie stood up too. She looked haggard, older than her years and her skin hadn't regained its colour all day.

"Ms Lawrence, Mr -" he checked his notes.

"Call me Alex."

"Alex," the surgeon smiled at him. "Lucy is in recovery and is doing well. Shall we sit?" He indicated to the seats behind the standing pair. They all sat. "We took an MRI of Lucy's back, there was no severe damage, some bruising to the skin and the muscles, nothing major internally." Maggie took Alex's hand and squeezed it. "Her right wrist is broken, again?" he raised his eyebrows.

Alex nodded, "In a previous attack."

The surgeon winced, "We have put it in a cast."

"Her face?" Maggie spoke up, "What about her face?"

"Yes. That was a little trickier. We straightened the break to her nose and managed to pin the largest breaks in her cheek bone and her eye socket. There was, thankfully no damage to her eye, she was -" he paused trying to find the right words, "Well no, *she* wasn't lucky but her eye was." he nodded, satisfied with how he had worded that. "We removed some small fragments of bone from the inside of her cheek. There is considerable bruising and swelling to her face and some external grazes which we have dressed."

"Will she have any scarring visible on her face?" Maggie's eyes pleaded.

119

"We were able to pin the cheekbone to the side of her nose from inside her mouth," he pointed into his mouth above the top teeth. "And to this bone here," he pointed with his finger to the outside corner of his own eye, "From a small incision just below her hairline. We are confident that there will be little to no visible scarring."

Maggie breathed a sigh of relief. She didn't want Lucy to be reminded of this ordeal every time she looked in the mirror.

The surgeon continued, "Lucy will need to stay in for a little while so that we can keep an eye on her. The damage to, in effect, her head, could cause further complications and so we would like to keep her hooked up to some monitors in the meantime." He stood up, ready to leave. As soon as she is out of recovery, I will ask the nurses to take you straight to her."

"Thank you." Alex held out his hand to the surgeon who shook it and walked back down the corridor.

Alex took his phone out of his pocket again and text his mum.

Out of theatre. Cheek bone had to be pinned ffs. Minimal scarring thankfully.

Oh and police have CCTV

At last Alex seemed to relax and settled down on a chair closing his eyes. Maggie picked up her bag, "Coffee Alex?"

"Tea please, just milk." He opened his eyes and smiled at her, "Thanks."

She nodded and wandered down to the drinks machine.

The next few days passed in a blur. Maggie and Alex took shifts at the hospital sitting with Lucy and when they couldn't be, Lucy knew that there was an officer outside her room. She was understandably afraid to be alone. Alex had put his studies temporarily on hold and his tutor was fully in agreement with a short sabbatical due to his mitigating circumstances. He did however need to work and so he worked from home every day between nine and five and spent every evening at the hospital reading to Lucy. He read her favourite books, women's health magazines, cheesy articles in any magazines that was lying around.

She would lie with a smile on her face, not a whole face smile which hurt her face. But her mouth smiled. And she held his hand with her not broken one, his thumb caressing the back of hers. From time to time when he arrived, Penny would already be there and the two of them thick as thieves.

He listened in at the door.

"It's beautiful Lucy!"

"I haven't chosen my veil yet, but I'm thinking long, like to my waist?" Lucy was mastering speaking without moving her face too much and she was managing quite well on the whole.

"Yeah, that would work great for the photo you want with you both kissing under it." Penny sniggered and added, "But just check it isn't too much for him to lift over your head. I mean, you don't want him getting tangled up in it." They both laughed at this.

"Ouch, don't make me laugh, my face hurts."

"Sorry," Penny almost snorted out loud which only started them off again.

Alex walked into the side room, "Now, now ladies," he faked a stern voice, "We have a sick patient here, we should not be having this much fun." He leant over the bed and planted a kiss on the side of Lucy's mouth avoiding her nose and cheek and then he put his hand on Penny's shoulder and enquired about school.

"Same old, same old. Plan, teach, mark, repeat! Everyone has been asking about Lucy though," she turned her attention to Lucy. "They were really worried about you, I was worried about you," she squeezed Lucy's hand.

"Ah, it's all cosmetic," Lucy spoke up, almost a ventriloquist. "I may look shit for now, but I'll mend," she smiled at Penny.

Alex and Penny shared an unnoticed glance at each other as Lucy gently rubbed her face, smiling hurt today. There was something niggling at the back of her mind. She had been trying to figure it out all day. It was annoying her in the same way that a missing jigsaw puzzle piece would annoy a child.

"The police came in again today," she looked at Alex. "Asking me again what happened and if there was anything I had remembered since."

"Was there?"

"Not yet. But I feel like I'm missing something," she frowned and then winced and then put her hand up to her face.

"It'll come back to you," he assured her.

"Well, now that you are here," Penny looked up at Alex, "I will head off. I have a bag of marking in the car that *has* to be done tonight."

"Thanks for coming to see me."

"Next time, I hope you'll be at home where the proper teabags are!" she laughed. "These machine made brews suck ass!"

She leant over and kissed Lucy on the forehead. "Keep getting better."

"I will."

After Penny had left the room, Alex sat down and buried his head in the bed next to Lucy, enjoying the warmth of her body, "I miss having you at home."

"I miss being at home too. I miss being able to do things for myself. I want to make myself a snack when I'm hungry and I miss watching Netflix," she laughed out loud, "Ouch!" her hand flew up to her nose which she carefully cradled.

They sat, her in bed, him next to her for the next hour or so. Alex's told her about his day and asked about the food Lucy had been served, which today had been satisfactory. They watched the visitors on the ward just outside the door and made up stories about them. It was clear to Alex that Lucy was tired and he needed to go shopping so he kissed her once more, plumped her pillow and made sure she was warm enough. He promised to come again tomorrow after work and then headed out. Lucy rolled onto her left side and closed her eyes.

That night she dreamt.

She relived the attack.

Her nightmare trapped her for the entirety of her beating. She watched his face in front of her, his mouth moving. Ears ringing, she couldn't hear his voice. She focussed on his mouth, the shape of the words he spoke; the look of hate in his eyes, the way he spat one of the words.

"You'll pay for what he did."

The word he spat was the word *'he'* which was spoken with such venom that Lucy felt it in her gut. That hatred drove this man to do what he was doing to her. Those words confirmed in Lucy's mind that these *were* targeted attacks and they wouldn't stop because *he*, Alex, had done something to upset someone.

She woke up, sun streaming through the window. There were tears rolling down her face and her heart was breaking.

Chapter 13

The police were at her bedside within twenty seven minutes of her dialling the officer from her mobile. She knew that because she watched every single minute pass. In that time, she had, not ignored, but not read three messages from Alex. She needed to focus. Inside her head she was trying to rationalise what this piece of information meant; to her and to their relationship. On the one hand, she needed to know what Alex had done. Had he broken the law? Was it related to his job? Computer people would probably know how to hack into bigger systems. Had he interfered in someone's livelihood? Uncovered something that made someone feel threatened? Was he blackmailing someone?

Did he even know that he *had* done something? Because if he did, could he have prevented it? Then the counter argument threw itself into the mix. If he knew that he had upset someone, then he would have known that her getting beaten up was his fault. How could he then stay in a relationship with her, knowing that she was taking these beatings because of him? How could he tell her in one breath that he loved her and wanted to spend the rest of his life with her and then allow that to happen to her? It was seriously fucked up.

Her mind was racing at a million miles an hour. At one point, she had to press her call button and get the nurse to sit with her and calm her down.

"Do you want something for your anxiety? I can ask the doctor to prescribe something for you."

"Yes please. But I need a clear head for when the police get here – so I won't take anything until after, if that's okay."

"Absolutely."

"Can you sit with me when they arrive? I don't want to do this alone – and I don't want Alex or my mum here."

"Let me just let the nurse station know that and then I will be right back."

The nurse left the room, closing the door behind her and Lucy could see that she was walking more briskly than usual. This was Lucy's favourite nurse, she was a similar age had the knack of calming her. If the police had to come at all, Lucy was glad that it was today.

There was a knock at the door and the nurse brought the CID officers in. There were two of them and they introduced themselves sat down at the side of the bed. The weight of what she was about to say and what might happen because of it made Lucy well up and she started to cry. The nurse sat down next to Lucy and held her hand.

Noticing her tears the female officer asked, "Are you happy to talk to us Lucy, we're here because you asked us to. Because you have remembered something?"

"Yes."

"Which attack is it regarding?"

"This one," Lucy moved her now cast hand towards her face to indicate that it was the attack that had resulted in how she was looking today.

"Okay, can you start from the beginning for us so that we can get a full picture?" the male officer's voice was reassuring.

And so Lucy went through the events of the day of her third beating. It was fairly straightforward until Lucy got to the newest piece of information.

"He told me that I would pay for what Alex had done," she cried inconsolably as she said it.

The officer was writing it all down. "Lucy, what were his exact words?"

"You'll pay for what *he* did." She spoke the word *he* in the same manner he's uttered it.

Lucy broke down again, the nurse was squeezing her hand, reassuring her and wiping her tears away.

"Thank you Lucy, we will look into this," the male officer stood up first.

"Can I suggest that you let us speak to Alex before you do?" the female officer stood up as well.

Tears streaming down her face, Lucy nodded. She knew how much this was going to hurt Alex. "Please speak to him today," she sobbed, "I need to see him."

There were no promises, "We'll be in touch."

"Thank you for this," the officer shook the notebook that he had been writing in. Then they were gone, the nurse showing them out and Lucy was alone.

***

"I should be able to get it finished today," Alex told his boss over the call.

"Make sure you get a break and finish on time this evening, you've better things to do than work straight through."

"Yeah, it shouldn't be a problem."

"Tomorrow's deadline can be moved if needed, it's just a loose one."

"Thanks Pete, I appreciate it."

"Talk later Alex, bye," and he hung up.

Taking a swig of his lukewarm cup of tea, gross, and another bite of his toast, Alex clicked his way through the open files on his computer desktop. When he was satisfied that he had everything open that he would need, he went to the kitchen to make himself another cup of tea. If he could get this work done today, if freed him up all day tomorrow to spend the time with Lucy at the hospital in the hope that she would be discharged to come home.

She'd had a shit time lately and he hoped that once this guy was caught they could live a long and happy life together. He stirred in the milk and looked out of the window. A car had just pulled up and two people were making their way to the door of his flat. They knocked at the door and he answered it.

"Hi?" he questioned

They both held out warrant cards and introduced themselves as CID involved in the investigation.

"Has he been caught?"

"Who?"

Alex pulled a 'why are you asking' face, "The guy who beat up Lucy," he raised his eyebrow in confusion to their question and the need for his answer. They walked into the living room and Alex sat, they didn't.

"There's been a development," the male officer spoke first.

Alex leant forward, eager to know.

"We've just come from the hospital after talking to Lucy," the female officer continued. "She remembered something."

"Great! What now?" Alex was enthusiastic at the possible developments and he stood up.

"Alex," the male officer spoke again, "What do you do for a living?"

"I write software and programs for computers."

"Is it possible to, shall we say," he looked at Alex, "aggravate people, in you line of work?"

"I don't think so. The boss gives me a job, I do it. If I don't my boss tells me to get it done. I don't really work with other people. Why do you ask?" Alex was now perched on the edge of the armchair.

"Lucy has remembered something that the perpetrator said to her before he walked away." She looked at the personal notebook that her colleague was holding open for her to read, "You'll pay for what he did."

"Alex, is it possible that someone is hurting Lucy to get back at you?" the male officer asked pointedly.

"What the hell?" Alex was standing up again now, his tall lanky frame filling the window area. "No." His hands were ragging through his hair, his face suddenly ashen. The thought that he could be the reason that his beautiful girl was lying in hospital made him feel physically sick. He heard the officers, but couldn't really focus on what it meant.

"It's really important that you tell us anything you can think of." Him.

"Anyone that might hold a grudge." Her.

"Any work that you've done that might have knocked someone's nose out of place." Him.

"Any recent fall outs?" Her.

Alex was leaning on the window sill now. Looking outside. "I work in my office upstairs, I see no one, speak to two, maybe three people about work," I can't think of anything." He started to put on his shoes that were lay at the side of the sofa. "I need to see Lucy."

The officers moved to block his path. "We have to request that you don't, unfortunately."

The female officer continued, "She has been brutally beaten and until we can be sure that there is no link, that something else won't happen -"

The male finished the sentence, "We need you to stay away from the hospital until we are sure that you are not the cause of her harm." It was as blunt as that.

At that, Alex crumpled back down to the sofa. Head in hands. Visibly upset.

"Can we get you anything before we leave Alex?"

He didn't reply.

"Well, if you think of anything, please call us." she placed a card on the table.

"We'll see ourselves out."

And with that, they were gone.

Alex didn't move for quite a while and then, when he regained some sense of self, he headed upstairs to his office. He turned his calendar back to the month before he met Lucy and looked through all the work he had been doing. Most of it small projects for clients, lots of little jobs for his boss, a couple of better paid pieces but nothing big enough to warrant a grudge and then the project that had earned him his bonus at Christmas. He screamed and punched the wall in frustration. If it was indeed linked to his work, he was glad he had taken Lucy away for Christmas. At least they had spent some quality time together. How would she feel about being with him if he had been the reason behind her pain?

He typed a quick and informal email to his boss.

Pete,

Police have asked me if anyone holds a grudge against me at work. They think Lucy is in hospital because someone is trying to hurt me. Any unhappy clients?

Project will be late. Head mashed.

Alex.

He got the customary 'unavailable' message as reply. Pete had that set as standard whether he was at his desk or skiing. You never knew when he would reply. Alex hoped that there wasn't a link to him. But equally, he was desperate for answers.

He spent the rest of the day doing absolutely nothing; not even moving from the sofa. He couldn't imagine his life without Lucy and to be frank, he didn't want to.

Chapter 14

Rachel lay on the mattress clutching her chest, she was sure that there was a broken rib this time.

"Drug her," the guy in jeans and a shirt, Azim, was saying. "She's more – pleasant – when she's quiet." As he said *pleasant* he flourished his hands.

He didn't like it when she said no to him and she said it a lot. In fact, she hadn't said yes to anything he'd requested. She was costing him valuable time and money. The other girls were bringing back 300 quid a night and she hadn't left this room yet.

Azim walked out of the room and another man entered. If Rachel hadn't been in pain, she would have kicked her feet around to keep him away, but she couldn't move thanks to the smack across the chest she'd just taken. Winded, she pressed her lips together determined not to have anything forced on her. This man was bigger, broader and fatter. He pinned her down easily. "This won't hurt at all," he grinned.

Instead of trying to put anything in her mouth like she had been expecting, she saw a needle in his hand. *Shit*. He had one of his fat legs over both of hers and no matter how hard she struggled, she wasn't going anywhere. He pressed the needle against the top of her foot and dug the needle between the toes. He removed the weight of his leg from hers and as the blood flow restarted, she felt the effect of the drugs almost immediately. She felt more at peace - as usual when the drugs were in her system. All of the stresses of her current life faded away and she looked at Jen. She lay, staring and thinking, the thoughts allowing themselves to fill her head unhindered.

Jen, wasn't her real name just the name she had adopted here. She'd worked in this place the longest. She was gifted nice clothes and shoes, was allowed to leave the room and visit the other girls that lived here. Jen had accepted that this was her life now and, to be fair, having arrived in the country in the back of a lorry, she was just glad to have a roof over her head and food to eat. She didn't talk much about her life before, whether that was because she couldn't remember much or because it made her sad, Rachel didn't know. Jen worked the streets at night, having sex for money which she brought back to Azim. There were other girls here who, instead of walking the streets, stayed here to entertain the men who Azim brought back for the services of the girls. It was grim work but the girls preferred it to being beaten.

Now that Rachel was incapacitated, Azim had returned to the room. He knelt down next to her and roughly grabbed her by the hair. "You will be making me some money tonight. If I have to drug you, I will."

There was no fight left, Rachel squeezed her eyes shut and a tear rolled sideways to her ear and into her hair. "There's a good girl." Azim left the room. "Have her ready for 7 p.m. and be prepared to make her more," he paused, "amenable if you have to."

Time passed and Rachel, now working for Azim, was dead on the inside. When she didn't 'perform' she was drugged and men would do whatever they wanted to her. When she wasn't drugged, she wished she was.

"Out Jen," Azim's voice ripped through the quiet one morning. Jen put down her magazine and left the room without batting an eyelid. "You want to do a nice job for me Rachel?"

Rachel rolled her eyes and looked him straight in the eye.

"I have a very special client," he showed her a picture on his phone. "Wants a white girl who scrubs up well." He looked at her. "We can get you some nice clothes and," he lifted his hands to her hair and she flinched expecting him to yank it like usual, "do something with these curls?"

Her mind, free from drugs for once, had moment of clarity. He was offering her the chance to get out of here? Accept it Rachel, nod your head her consciousness was on high alert. She nodded her head. "You have to behave though." She continued to look at him, expressionless. "And you'll need a new name. Trixie works, yes?" Rachel shrugged.

An hour later, Jen was brushing her hair with warm water and spraying it with something that smelt like coconut. Then she sat and twisted each curl back into place with her fingers.

Rachel was given a white dress to wear, and a pair of gold heals.

"Azim is making a lot of money tonight. Make sure you behave or he will kill you." Jen whispered. "If you try to run. He will find you. He's done it before and he will do it again."

Rachel's blood ran cold. Disappointment flooded her hopes, she knew it was true. The girls that no longer worked here hadn't been 'allowed' to just leave. Chances were, they were at the bottom of a canal or in the landfill. She nodded slowly. She knew she had to come back, at least for now.

That night, she dressed and Jen helped her with her makeup. Red lipstick and plenty of mascara. She caught sight of her reflection in the glass and she saw a glimpse of her life before, holding her phone high for a selfie to celebrate her love for life and the prospect of another notch on her bedpost. She hung her head in shame at the life she had wished herself into. She used to love her life, she'd loved the sex, not anymore. The thought of men's hands on her body once made her smile, that had turned to disgust and now, she was numb to it all. Azim came in to collect her. He was 'delivering' her himself. She sat in the back seat of his car as he drove her through the streets to a carpark in the middle of nowhere.

"Need anything to get you 'happy?'" he asked her. He often offered his girls drugs to help them have a good night.

She shook her head, she'd been dangerously close to being reliant on the drugs over the past weeks and when she had realised how she was becoming addicted, she'd battled to get a clear head again. It had taken every ounce of what little strength she had left to stop herself kicking off just to be drugged again.

"Go make *him* happy," he flashed his lights and pointed to a blue BMW that had responded with a similar flash of lights.

Rachel got out of the car and carefully walked across the street to the car. The passenger window was rolled down and she could see a man, mid-forties, receding hair line but clearly wealthy and hopefully fairly kind. She opened the door and got in the car.

Azim picked her up in the small hours of the morning and she handed him the envelope that she knew contained money.

"Good girl," he patted her leg, his hand lingering a little too long on the bare flesh. She held her breath until he removed it.

Azim was kinder to Rachel after that night. He bought her some shampoo and let her use the bath in the flat above. He bought her magazines and puzzle books. One time he even bought her chocolate biscuits which she shared with Jen.

"See, it's not so bad, is it?"

"Not so bad? Are you kidding me?" Rachel glared at Jen. "I was drugged and raped for weeks." She took the packet of biscuits back from Jen and took one out for herself, softening her face, "But, yes. This is better than it was." She tried to make her smile genuine.

"Sorry." Jen hung her head. "That never happened to me."

"I don't want to talk about it. Let's eat all of these though! Before anyone else finds out we have them!" Rachel spread the biscuits out on the cover of the magazine in front of her. The girls smiled and ate. It was one of the better afternoons they had.

Azim took Rachel to the BMW man three times over the next fortnight.

The guy was bearable. He wasn't much of a talker; a computer guy judging by the monitors and towers stacked up under the desk that was set up as his work station. She knew not to ask questions and to do what was requested of her. He didn't have a wife or a girlfriend, he'd told her. Too busy for the commitment, the hassle. Preferred the pay-as-you-go arrangement as he put it.

The sex wasn't good, but neither was it bad. He didn't make her do too much that she wasn't comfortable with – well apart from the whole prostitution thing – but she didn't really have a choice when it came to that. He just wanted sex without having to go out and find someone. He didn't want to know about her. He just wanted a girl to bend over and fuck.

One night, Azim brought a woman back to the flats. She seemed to know him well – well enough that he took her into one of the rooms to shag her. Her name was Melody, long legs, long hair. Jen mentioned that she thought she was a high end escort. And by the looks of the clothes and the jewellery she was wearing, Rachel had to agree. She started to spend quite a bit of time with Azim, making it quite clear that she was interested in Rachel. Azim steered the subject elsewhere and sent Rachel to her room every time Melody came around. Jen had her suspicions.

"She wants you to go and work for her," she whispered one evening as they sat on the mattress, "But because Azim makes so much money from you now, she'll have to pay big bucks to get you."

"What? Pay what exactly?"

"Well how much does BMW man pay for you? A grand? More?"

"I don't know that!" Rachel's eyes were wide.

"Don't you ever look and see?"

"No!" Rachel had never even considered it. A grand? A night? That was an insane amount of money to spend on sex. BMW guy was averaging three grand a month. She laughed out loud.

"What are you laughing at?"

"BMW guy would be better off getting a girlfriend! More sex and cheaper too." The girls both laughed at the absurdity that was their reality.

Then Jen's face was serious, "Azim gets paid three grand a month if he keeps you. He won't sell you to anyone for less than twenty."

Rachel paled, twenty grand? The realisation made her feel sick. Never mind Azim not selling her. The smallest plan in the back of her mind that she might one day escape fizzled. She was never going to get out.

The new knowledge added a sense of fear for Rachel. What if BMW man stopped asking for her? What if Azim earned more money from one of the other girls? He wouldn't need her anymore. What then? Was she disposable?

Thankfully, she needn't have worried. Another client to add to BMW man came along the next week and Rachel was now the highest paid of Azim's girls. He allowed her to choose clothes from a website which he then bought for her.

One evening, as she waited in Azim's car for her ride to arrive, she thought that he seemed restless. "I'll pick you up in three hours," he said.

She looked at him, he'd never given her a time before. He would usually have the client dictate the length of time, but she didn't argue. She smiled and nodded. She had just taken off her seatbelt when he swore, "FUCK!"

Before she knew what was happening, he had put the car into reverse, spun around in the carpark and was speeding off. She tried to look over her shoulder to see what it was, but the speed at which he was driving and the sharp turns he was taking were sending her all over the passenger seat. She fought with the seatbelt to try and get it back around her but every time she tried, he would turn another corner and the seatbelt would lock. She was panicked. He was driving dangerously. More erratically than usual. On a straight bit of road, she managed to wedge her feet into the foot well, straighten herself on the seat and pull the seatbelt around her. Once clicked in place, she felt safer, even though she was terrified at his driving frenzy.

"Azim?" she questioned.

"Police," he replied without looking at her. "I think we shook them."

She looked over her shoulder and breathed a sigh of relief.

As she turned around she heard a scream, a mother's scream. Her eyes locked with those of a child. A boy. No more than seven years old. In a split second he was on and then off the bonnet.

Azim hit the brakes. "SHIT."

The car screamed, swerved and crashed into another vehicle. There was a loud bang and Rachel was aware of her face making contact with something hard. Then everything went black.

Chapter 15

When Rachel opened her eyes, she couldn't see anything. The world was white. What was that noise? There was a ringing noise, deafening. Something was digging into her leg. It hurt. She tried to look around her, but all she could see was white. First she tried to turn her head to the left. Nope, she couldn't. Then she tried to turn her face to the right. Some movement, but ouch, that hurt. She was leaning forward on something. It was digging into her chest but it held her weight and she was happy to relinquish to it. She closed her eyes.

She tried to remember how she got here. Where was *here*? The ringing seemed further away now. She opened her eyes again, trying to see anything. A tingling sensation, that was new, she moved her fingers. There was something just out of her reach, the very tips of her fingers were barely touching it, and it felt warm. She struggled, stretching her fingers far enough in the hope that she would be able to reach whatever it was. The pain in her left shoulder was the next thing that she was aware of. She made a mental list of everything she could feel. Sore left leg, sore left shoulder and a pain across her chest, limited and painful movement in her neck. She listed everything else that she knew. There was a lot of white, a ringing sound – which was now almost gone and something warm just in front of her right hand. Time had slowed down, it seemed.

Once again, she closed her eyes and tried to recall where she was. Nothing. She couldn't remember anything. Panic rose in her throat. She threw her arms out sideways making contact with something soft on her right and something hard on her left. Left hand turned palm outwards she moved her hand around in small circles, getting her bearings. The second her hand met the shape the handle, she worked out that she was in a car. Suddenly desperate to get out she yanked on it. As she did so, a ripping sensation in her leg made her scream out in anguish. It was the most pain she had ever felt. Once she started screaming, she couldn't stop. She was trapped in a car. Trapped and blind. Her hands went up to the ceiling and out towards the window, she was banging and screaming and calling out in desperation for help.

Out on the street, in the moments following the accident, the focus was not yet on the car and its occupants but on the body of the boy. The police had arrived first, almost as if they were already in the area. Paramedics were lifting the stretcher and wheeling it back to the ambulance where a man and a woman huddled together and climbed inside. The blue lights came on as another ambulance spun around the corner.

Police officers and paramedics were running towards the car and the woman screaming, speaking on radios as they did so.

"Hello, Miss?" someone knocked on the window "I'm a police officer, help is here."

"GET ME OUT!" Rachel screamed.

"Miss, calm down. I don't want to open the door until the paramedics have assessed things. But I am right here. Try not to move."

"I can't see!" The panic rose in her chest again, "I can't see anything! Get me out!"

"Miss, you've been in a car crash. We can't move you until the paramedics and fire crew have assessed the situation. I am right outside the window."

Rachel put her hand up to the cool glass again. She spread her palm on the window and the police officer put her palm against it. Rachel felt the warmth and calmed a little.

"What is your name?"

Rachel thought hard. What was her name? She knew her name. So what was it?

"Miss? Are you okay? What's your name?" he repeated.

"I DON'T KNOW MY NAME." Rachel cried out.

"You're in shock, it will come back. Try to stay calm."

There were other voices outside now. Talking to each other and into radios. Rachel could hear people talking and moving around the car.

"We need another ambulance," the voice spoke from somewhere on her left, "Driver and passenger. Driver, male, needs urgent medical attention.

Rachel felt cool air blow in and around her legs as the driver's door was pulled open. She could hear the voices from outside the car much clearer now. "Can I get a crash bag NOW please?" someone shouted and then "I NEED A DOCTOR ON SITE,"

The paramedics pulled the driver out of the car and had started working on him.

"GET ME OUT!" Rachel screamed.

Another person climbed into the car. "Hi there, I'm Paul, a paramedic. I just need to see how you are and see how we can get you out of here. The police officer said that you can't see anything, is that right?"

"Yes, everything is white." Rachel started, "I don't know where I am, I can't remember anything." The panic started again but the paramedic sensed it and continued talking.

"That can happen, especially if you've got a concussion. Try to stay calm. I am just going to shine a light in your eyes." Rachel felt him leaning over her and heard a click, presumably a light being shone into her eyes. "So, can you tell me where you've got any pain?"

"My shoulder, the left one. It feels like something cutting into my chest. And my leg, something is digging into it and when I tried to open the door it was pulling my skin."

"Yep, I can see that." He had moved himself back into the driver's seat. "The pain across your chest is where the seatbelt has cut into your skin. Your dress hasn't really offered any cushioning so there is a wound that I need to dress. Is it okay if I get on with that?"

Rachel tried to nod her head, "Ouch," she muttered.

"Something else sore?"

"Yes, my neck. If I try to move it."

"Okay, we'll get you in a collar as well. Just give me a second to get what I need," he waited a second for her to register what he'd said, then he left the car and the cool evening breeze flooded the car again.

Rachel heard him talking as he walked away. She couldn't make out the words but the tone of his voice certainly didn't have a cheerful tone to it. Listening in to the other group of paramedics, those with the driver, it was clear that there was nothing they were able to do and that whoever had been in the car with her was dead. She tried to think who she was with. She couldn't remember anything. The paramedic had said she was in a dress, could she be in a taxi? Was she going out? If she was in a taxi, surely she'd be in the back? If it wasn't a taxi then she must know the man? But who was he? She had no idea.

There was a bit of a ruckus outside all of a sudden and the police officer's voice shouted, "Please sir, no pictures," and then "I SAID, NO PICTURES!" she heard feet running away. Rachel couldn't tell if anyone was running after whoever had taken the pictures but she didn't care right now.

The paramedic was now back in the car chatting to her in his soothing voice. He reminded her that he was going to clean and dress the wound on her chest. It stung, but she knew it needed doing and once it was done, they could work on getting her out.

"I'm going to put my hand on your shoulder and see what I can feel, is that okay?"

"Yes."

She felt the gloved hand move to the tip of her shoulder, "I need you to stay as still as you can until we get you out of here."

"I can move my arms fine, it just hurts," she started to say but was interrupted.

"Best to keep as still as you can until we can assess what you've done. Sometimes the adrenaline can give the effects of pain relief."

She felt his fingers walking along the top of her shoulder towards her neck.

"Ouch!" she cried out.

"Yeah, you've possibly got some damage to your clavicle. There is a bit of a lump."

"Mm hmm," she muttered.

"I need to give you some pain relief so that we can get you out of the car, okay?"

She sighed. She didn't care what she needed, she just wanted to be out of this car. She wanted to remember what the hell she was doing in the car, who she was with and where she was going. But she couldn't remember a bloody thing. It was like someone had removed her memories entirely.

The paramedic was back and asking, "Do you know of any allergies?"

"I can't remember a fucking thing about me," she grumbled. It was so frustrating

"It's okay, I still have to ask."

She smiled.

He took her hand, "Sharp scratch," she gritted her teeth as she felt the needle go in. He taped it in place and then she heard him rummaging then some pressure and something cold passing through the needle into her arm. "Morphine," he said.

She closed her eyes and he stepped out of the vehicle to speak to the fire and rescue team that were standing outside the car.

The paramedic beckoned to a colleague to get into the car to monitor the girl and he moved the rescue team to the back end of the car. "Her leg is compressed, wedged between the seat and the side of the car which has crumpled inwards. There is a compound fracture and I can't see it fully, but I think a partial amputation – she mentioned a pulling sensation. I won't be able to see properly until we get the door off and it could well be attached to her and need to come with us."

It took an hour to remove Rachel from the wreck. She was taken to hospital. The same hospital as the driver, pronounced dead at the scene, and the boy, who had died from his injuries in the ambulance.

***

The hospital chapel was deathly quiet and empty except for a woman sat in the far corner, leaning against the wall. Her face was that of disbelief, too much to take in, in too short a time. She felt as though it was a dream, happening to someone else. Numbness was taking over every part of her. Except her heart, that felt the enormity of, and knew the reality of what had happened today. Her heart so broken, it might as well be ripped from her chest. She was not the same person anymore.

A man sat on the floor of the smoker's shelter outside the hospital doors. A cigarette burning out, unsmoked in his hand. Life destroyed in a moment. How does anyone get over something like this? He never would. He would never get over what had happened today. It would live with him for the rest of his life; he would find the person responsible for tearing his family apart and he would kill them. In his pocket, his phone beeped, signalling the arrival of a text. He unlocked it to see a photo of the car that had killed his son, the paramedic and passenger and on the road besides, the driver.

In between the ambulances, a young paramedic was crouched down. Her head resting on her knees, she wept. New to the job and the first time she had been involved in a child's death. She wanted her mum to hold her and tell her everything would be okay.

In theatre, surgeons worked to save a woman's leg. A woman who did not know who she was, or how she came to be in that car. In the morgue a man's body was being photographed and prepared for the fridge, a post-mortem scheduled for morning.

At the crash scene, the car was being lifted onto the back of a truck - evidence. And police officers, who had been actively seeking the driver, were trying to piece together what they could from the amount of cash, drugs and the number of mobile phones that were found in the boot of the black car.

The neighbourhood was in mourning for the loss of life in their quiet, highly sought after residence.

Still in shock, Megan and Michael took a taxi home from the hospital in the small hours of the morning. They didn't talk once. In fact, very little was spoken by either of them for the next few days. Megan often sat in her armchair, sometimes she would watch the world go by and the other times she would grow so irritated with the scenes of normality that she saw that she would close the curtains. As the days passed and once the funeral was a sorrowful memory for most people, Megan spent more and more time upstairs. Lying on her bed, she would stare at the ceiling. She tried to read but when the characters in her books were happier than her, she resented them and when they were miserable, she cursed them for having no real reason for feeling so.

Michael spent the days watching and re-watching the news. He now knew who the deceased driver was, Muhammad Azim Khan, 32 years old, originally from Bradford and known to the police. But the girl, there had been no information given in any of the reports about her. He would scroll through the internet hoping to find a clue to who she was: all he had was the photograph on his phone. She still had her life and that bothered him. She would no doubt move on with her life whilst his, and Megan's hung in time. Unable to accept that the blame lay solely with the driver and he was dead, he became hell bent on finding her. He would make her pay.

Chapter 16

Alex sat on the mats at the climbing wall. He was getting frustrated with a climb that he should have been able to do but the truth of the matter was, since he and Lucy had gotten together, he had climbed less, eaten more and had found more pleasure in spending time with her than with the lads, the gritstone or the plywood.

However, being home alone was boring. He had taken some entitled holiday from work to get his head straight and this was his third consecutive day here. It was nice to do something that required little thinking about what was going on in the rest of his life. Air pods in and chalked up, off he went. He had climbed all the easy routes and now he was trying a V6 that was testing him. His fingers knew it and burned. He clenched and unclenched them a few times to get the blood flowing again. He'd already spent a good ten minutes trying and another five sitting staring at it. The wall mocked him, he knew the move he needed to master but his muscles cried in protest when he tried. He resolved to have one last try and then head home. Maybe today was the day that the police would call and tell him that they had found the man and that there was no link to him. His mobile beeped and he grabbed it hoping it was Lucy; it was Chris.

Hey man, Carl says you're at the wall?

Was about to finish up and head home soon…

Give me 20 mins and I'll be there.

OK.

Carl, Chris and Alex had climbed together since junior school, they had spent all their school holidays here at the climbing wall. They brought girlfriends through their high school years, mostly to get a good look at their backsides as they tried to climb - he chuckled inwardly to himself. Between the three of them, they had introduced many new climbers to the wall.

As they all headed to university, they had continued to climb albeit in different climbing centres around the country and chose to spend any free time that coincided, on climbing holidays in the lakes, in Scotland and in France. It would be good to see Chris again.

Alex thought back to the last time he had been here. Lucy had been with him, well, she was in the café, drinking Latte and eating the homemade brownies and reading a book whilst he climbed. Now that his mind had wandered towards Lucy he couldn't get it back onto the climb, his heart sank and he sighed. He took off his shoes and walked barefoot to the edge of the mat to find his rucksack and his water bottle. He wished that thinking about Lucy wouldn't get him so down. It wasn't as if they weren't still together, they were yet being unable to see her in person made it feel awkward. He spoke to Maggie most days who told him medically how Lucy was doing. She was healing. Alex didn't speak with Lucy on the phone, but they did text most evenings.

Alex had agreed with the police on this one. As much as it broke his heart, until he knew that Lucy spending time with him wasn't going to cause her to get beaten, they should continue to stay apart. This was only the fourth day and it was excruciating. Still, he would not cause her anymore harm.

"Hey! Is that you, Alex?" a female voice called from the wall behind him.

He turned and smiled, "Hannah, long time! What have you been up to?"

"Ah, I'm just here visiting my mum and catching up with Kerry," she nodded back at the wall where her sister was halfway up a tricky climb.

"She got good!" Alex mused.

"You heading off?" she nodded towards his bare feet.

"Chris is heading over so I guess I'll hang on for a bit longer."

She smiled. He smiled. She was still pretty, even with chalk smudged on her forehead and around the edges of her woolly hat. "Might see you on the wall then?" she raised her eyebrows and went back to Kerry where she proceeded to check him out over her shoulder; her one-time, almost, semi-serious yet non-committal boyfriend.

Alex shook his head. There was a time when he would have been all over that, he stopped his mind from wandering and mentally undressing her. "Not today," he sighed.

By the time Chris arrived, Alex was in the café area and had ordered some chips. He hadn't eaten well in the last few days. His once-loved pastime of cooking had become something he did for Lucy's pleasure and without her at home, there had been no point. He'd even phoned a takeaway the night before last.

"Hey man! You look good!" Alex smiled, Chris did look good. He had lost a couple of pounds and was clean shaven. "Where did the beard go?" Alex laughed.

"Women find me sexier without it," Chris winked and laughed.

"You seeing anyone?"

"One? There's an interesting prospect."

Alex rolled his eyes, "Same old, same old."

"Why get tied down when you can see who you want, when you want?" His eyes wandered to the plate of chips on the table. "You're done climbing then?"

"Yeah, Hannah was in." He rolled his eyes.

Chris laughed, "Fair play."

They sat and talked for the next hour, Alex telling Chris about Lucy, about the beatings, their engagement and the fact that the police thought someone might be trying to get back at him by attacking her.

"Oh, that's shit man, really shit," Chris agreed. "So what now?"

"I have to wait until the police are satisfied that I am not the cause of Lucy's attacks and then I can get back to planning a wedding with her!" he smiled. Saying that out loud made him feel ten times better than he had been feeling.

"Great! I will look forward to the invite then," he grinned at Alex. "But for now, climbing. You say Hannah is here? What about her sister?" He stuck his tongue into the inside of his cheek and pulled face.

Alex just groaned and shook his head. "Go man, just go!"

Chris patted him on the shoulder as he left the café and Alex ate his chips whilst scrolling through Facebook on his phone. Automatically, he checked the local police Facebook page. He found the post he was looking for. An e-fit of the man who had attacked Lucy with the warning not to approach as he could be dangerous and had already attacked women (a woman, Alex mentally corrected the post) three times. It wasn't the actual post that interested Alex, it was the comments. Reading them made him feel like he was doing something useful. There were over a hundred comments and he scrolled them all as he ate. Nothing of interest yet. Then, finished with Facebook and with his chips, he put on his coat headed out of the door and back to the car.

As his phone connected to the car, it started ringing: his boss.

"Hey Pete,"

"Alex," he was walking, Alex could hear it in his voice. "I've just popped out of the office to talk to you. Is now a good time to talk?"

"Yeah, I'm in the car."

"Driving?" Pete questioned.

"No."

"Don't set off just yet, let me talk first. You need to hear this." Alex could hear that he was out of breath and wondered if he had just run down the flight of stairs as he could now hear traffic on the street. "Right. I looked into what you asked me. About the grudge," he paused.

"Uh-huh?"

"Well, do you remember Jon, that guy from Astra-Tech – start of last year? The one who we were dealing with initially - on the Burton system, but then you preferred to speak to Sharon so she took over dealing with the account?"

Alex shrunk an inch at the mention of her name. That had gotten testy, you could say. Started fun, soon wasn't and he couldn't get shot of her for weeks. It was just before he'd met Lucy.

Pete continued, "Did you two, err – excuse my lack of professionalism here - did you shag her?"

Alex wished he wasn't having this conversation, he was pretty sure that it was in his contract that he had to declare relationships with clients, no matter how brief. "Err, Yes. Once."

"That's what I thought. Did you know that she was married?"

Again, the shame crept up Alex's neck, "Ah, man, this is embarrassing." He rubbed his forehead. "I did know, yes."

"Well," he had stopped walking now and Alex could hear him catching his breath. "She is, or rather, *was* married to Jon. And, it seems that she quite enjoyed rubbing his nose in it. Mentioned you by name when they got divorced last summer."

Alex's blood froze. It literally stopped moving towards his heart, which promptly stopped and then started again.

"He sent an email to HR telling them that you lacked professionalism with client relationships and that he wanted you fired for misconduct – or else."

"What? Why wasn't I told this?"

"The email ended up in a spam folder. It wasn't until I requested all emails from the last years' clients that we even saw it."

"Shit."

"Yeah."

"I'd better let the police know."

Chapter 17

2017

Rachel was sat up in bed eating a sandwich, which had been brought for her lunch, and watching daytime television on the small personal TV in front of her. It had been almost two weeks since the accident that had brought her here and although she was beginning to heal well, the amnesia was preventing the hospital staff from discharging her. On arrival at the hospital, the doctors had found her to be malnourished, dehydrated and they had noticed track marks on both of her arms and on one of her feet. Although there was no trace of drug use on any of the blood tests, the doctors had informed the police when they came for updates.

Her physical injuries from the accident were a broken collar bone, three fractured ribs, bruising and a laceration across her chest from the seatbelt during the crash. Her left leg had required skin grafts and several hours of reconstruction after part of the car door had been forced, by the impact, to cut into the muscle.

Rachel still couldn't remember who she was. Nor could she remember the man she had been with or where they were going.

The police had informed her that the driver of the vehicle, now deceased, had been known to them and had been under the influence of drugs - this was the probable cause of the accident but it was still vital that she try to remember anything she could, no matter how insignificant it seemed. Rachel couldn't remember anything before the accident. The most recent memory she could pull out of her useless brain was her birthday party and crazy night out with her best friend Sophie in the spring of last year. This in itself was concerning for her, but the medical professionals assured her that her memories would come back. It was a trauma reaction and that she would be okay.

"I wonder if Sophie knew where I was going. We always went out together," she spoke with sudden clarity and confidence one day when the police asked her. The words rolled off her tongue so easily that it was difficult to work out how she knew this.

The police officers shared a sideways glance at each other, for someone with amnesia, she was remembering a fair bit today, this was good. Perhaps she would start to remember more. "Do you have a number for Sophie?"

"No, but I know that she works at Café Rouge in the city centre." she smiled.

"We will check it out and see what your friend knows," the police officers shared a knowing look with each other. "Just on the off-chance, as you are remembering more today, can you remember what phone you had?"

"An iPhone 8," she furrowed her brow again at how she was able to recall that minor detail, but not her own name, "Was it in the car?"

"We can check the evidence file, did it have a case on it?"

"Yeah, silver glitter."

Rachel felt a flicker of hope as she recalled another minor detail from her life. The police assured her they would look into the whereabouts of her phone and left a card with their number, promising to let her know how they got on calling Sophie.

***

At her desk in the police station, Police Officer Blake had just come off the phone with Sophie. She rubbed her temples with her fingers and stretched her arms about her head. She wasn't sure how well this was going to go. The girl sounded a bit, well - thick - or perhaps hungover. She quickly called the Duty Sergeant to get an opinion and decide what to do next.

"I'll invite her here? Or to her local station?"

"Get her to come here. Get her to identify our girl from photos and then ask about the driver. She may have known him too.

"I'll get onto that now," Blake assured her boss.

"Let me know how you get on."

Three hours later, the most beautiful girl that Blake had ever seen walked through the doors and into the reception of the police station. Long blonde hair pulled into a bobble high on her head, brown eyes and the longest eyelashes. This girl would not have looked out of place on a catwalk. She was closely followed by a guy, wearing a jeans, leather jacket and a white t-shirt. They were a good looking couple. It made Blake feel like she should have made more effort, despite her uniform. Sophie, confidently walked to the desk.

"I was called here by Officer Blake."

"Name please?"

"Sophie Whitehall," she twitched and tapped her manicured nails on the desk, not in an impatient way, it was more an anxiety reaction to being in the police station. Blake had seen it many times. She did, however, hide her own nails away, disgusted at them in comparison.

"I am Officer Blake. Sophie, if you could come this way please."

The boyfriend found a seat and waited in the reception area. As they walked through the double doors and into a room off the main corridor Blake made small talk, "Have you travelled far?"

"Took about an hour on the train."

"Not local then?"

"Nah, Leeds."

Blake showed her into a small interview room, "If you'd like to take a seat," she indicated the comfier seats in the corner of the room. "I would like to show you a series of photographs of women to see if you can identify any of them as a person you have known in the past."

"What's this all about?" Sophie enquired.

"If you identify anyone, I'll be able to give you more details."

Sophie nodded.

Blake began to hand her photographs of various women they had on file. When Sophie saw her friend in a photo following her accident, she cried out. "Oh my God! She IS alive. I have been trying to get hold of her for months!"

"Who is this girl?" Blake asked.

"Rachel, Rachel Carnegie."

"And when was the last time you saw Miss Carnegie?"

"On a night out in December last year. She went home with a guy, and I went home with -" she nodded her head towards the door indicating the guy in the reception area.

"And you didn't see her after that?"

"No."

"And you haven't seen her or heard from her since then?

"No."

"Did you report her missing?"

"NO!" she seemed surprised at this.

"Why not?"

"She wasn't missing," she paused a moment, "Well I didn't realise she was. She was reading all my messages. I just assumed that she was too busy with her new guy to reply." She picked at her nails. "After a while, I thought that maybe I had pissed her off leaving her in the club that night, and she wasn't replying, so I stopped messaging her."

"Can I show you some other photographs?"

"Of Rachel?"

"No, I would like to see if you recognise any of these men as the man she was with that night."

Sophie nodded.

Blake set down some photos of men that had their photographs on file, including one of the driver. She watched Sophie's face carefully for any glimmer of recognition. Nothing.

"No, I don't recognise any of them."

"Thank you." Blake began to remove the photos from the table and Sophie began to talk.

"So, can I see Rachel? Is she okay?"

Blake had suspected that this question would come up and had already checked with her boss if she was allowed to divulge the name of the hospital Rachel was in, "Of course you can. She is in the City General, Ward 122."

"She's in hospital?"

"She is. Shall I call you a taxi?"

"Thank you." Sophie nodded.

"No problem." Blake replied.

***

Rachel scrunched her hair to keep the curls as they dried, smiling to herself. The nurses had helped her to have a shower and they'd washed her hair for her. She hadn't been able to stand under the hot water, hold on and wash her own hair – she still struggled with her injured leg, but a shower instead of a bed bath had been immensely good for the soul, even sat down, and with help. Sitting up on her bed, she pulled a magazine from the cupboard at the side of her bed and flicked through the pages but nothing caught her attention. She couldn't relate to any of the celebrities, didn't know what was happening in the soaps and the fashion pages didn't interest her. She put the magazine down and pulled the bedside television closer to her, daytime TV it was then. There was nothing more comforting than the little routine she'd developed and her everyday 'normality.'

Rachel couldn't see past the bed halfway down the ward, with the curtains pulled around but she assumed that the door at the end of the ward must have opened and closed again because there was a blast of warm air that filtered down to her bed at the far end. She was aware of footsteps, but they were heels and certainly not the clumpy footsteps of the police officers or the gentle squish of the nurse's shoes so she didn't look up until there was a gasp. A sharp intake of breath and then someone was flailing their arms and running up the side of her bed.

"Oh. My. God," the voice shrieked from somewhere behind her head. Somewhere, buried in Rachel's black curls was a blonde girl, who was, crying?

Rachel's initial panic subsided. This person knew her, and clearly cared about her. Looking to the foot of the bed, she saw a guy, standing with his hands in his pocket, not sure where to look and looking slightly uncomfortable at the display of emotion in front of him.

Chapter 18

She knew that they were coming today.

They had phoned ahead, which they didn't usually do so Lucy assumed they had something concrete to tell her.

"Lucy, how are you?" the female officer tilted her head to the right and smiled.

"I'm being discharged tomorrow," she beamed. "I *cannot* wait to sleep in my own bed!"

"We have an update for you," the female officer looked at the male officer who continued.

"We've found a likely link between the perpetrator," he paused, "and Alex."

"What?" Lucy was confused.

"It would appear that Alex may have rustled some feathers when he had a," he coughed, "a one night stand with a client's wife, early last year."

"Early last year?" she did the maths, "But we were together early last year?" Lucy closed her eyes, suddenly feeling unwell.

The female officer looked at Lucy, she had a look of sympathy in her eyes.

The male officer continued, "There was an email suggested that something bad would happen if Alex wasn't removed from his post and - well, as you know, Alex was not sacked."

Lucy started to cry. Alex? Had he slept with this woman whilst they were together? Had he cheated on her?

"Does Alex know that you are here?"

"It was Alex who came to the station to talk to us."

Lucy buried her head under the sheets and began to sob, "I'd like to be left alone now, please."

"Of course," the male officer started to walk towards the end of her bed.

The female hung around a second longer, "We will let you know if anything else transpires."

Once they were gone, Lucy called her mum and they both cried. Lucy, for being hurt and betrayed. Maggie, because her daughter's heart was breaking.

***

Maggie made the bed in Lucy's old bedroom and emptied the drawers so that Lucy could use them. Alex, being the gentleman he'd always been had put Lucy's clothes into a suitcase and brought them over. Maggie felt a bit sorry for him, he looked broken. He clearly felt the guilt of his actions almost killing Lucy and, as much as she should hate him for causing it, she couldn't. She hugged him on the doorstep before he'd had wandered back off to the car in the rain; his t-shirt sticking to his back as he slouched and slumped over the wheel.

Alex had made up his mind, before he'd even been to the police, that if he had been the cause of Lucy's trauma, then he would leave her to live her life. There was no way that he could be with her, living his best life knowing that he had caused her so much pain.

Lucy had made the decision a long time ago, back in the early days of their relationship, that if he ever cheated on her, and it sounded very likely now that he had, that she wanted nothing more to do with him. Maggie could read her daughter's face though, and she saw that the love Lucy felt for Alex even now, was causing her more pain than any of her physical injuries.

Alex nor Lucy had not spoken to each other. They were both hurting but Maggie for one, was glad that Alex was off the scene. She did *not* want her daughter being hurt again - seeing it happen had been the worst thing she'd ever experienced - and if Alex was the cause, regardless of how much pain and heartbreak followed, Lucy was safer away from him.

***

Alex started at the computer screen. He knew that work would occupy his mind, if only he could get started. He took a slug of his coffee and put his Air pods in his ears. The familiar, tuneful tones of the electric guitar filled his ears before the beat kicked in and the sound of Iron Maiden filled his head. If anything was going to keep his thoughts from lingering, heavy metal ought to do it. He pulled up the files to the project he should have finished the previous week and set about working on it. He logged onto the server and soon, he was in the zone.

Lunchtime came and went and he continued working, finding solace in the coding and lack of human interaction needed for his job. At 4:00 p.m. he emailed Pete.

Pete,

Uploaded the TLS project onto Server B.

Would appreciate feedback – Alex.

He headed to the kitchen, his stomach growling and his eyes bleary from the six and a bit hours of screen time. He didn't fancy anything in the fridge and couldn't be arsed with making anything that required any actual thought, so grabbed his coat and headed out to the pie shop at the end of the high street. If he was lucky they'd have something left, something warm and ready to eat.

The pie shop had sold out of everything decent so Alex had walked a bit further to the sandwich shop, which had closed at 2:00 p.m.

"Bugger," he swore under his breath. It was only now that he realised quite how hungry he was. He'd been running on adrenaline, caffeine and heavy metal all day. The chippy opened at 5:00 p.m. It was 4:30 p.m. now so he decided to grab a pint in The Oak and then get a chippy on his way home.

It had been ages since he's been in the pub, certainly not since he'd met Lucy – it was a quiet pub, serving food in the back room. It was homely and he relaxed with the first sip of his beer. What had happened to his life in such a short period of life time? He should be busy planning a wedding to the girl he loved and instead, she'd just been discharged from hospital after her third beating. And all because of him and a stupid, boyish need to get his leg over. He ordered another pint, and then another and before could stop it, he was wallowing in self-pity. A couple of girls came into the bar one of them flirted with the bar man before they were taken into the restaurant. He was envious of them for their simple lives and envious that they could have anyone they wanted. His love life was in tatters and even the thought of bed hopping with a fit young girl didn't appeal. He headed home, via the chippy. Ate, sulked and went to bed.

***

Lucy ate dinner with her mum. She didn't talk much. She hadn't talked much since she came home. Maggie wasn't too worried, there was a lot to process and as long as Lucy was eating, she would heal. Both her heart and her body. She had removed the engagement ring from her finger choosing instead to wear it on her necklace.

Thankfully Penny was coming round tonight. She promised to bring wine, cakes and a good film. Maggie smiled inwardly, it was exactly what Lucy needed and Maggie, would enjoy a good night's sleep without worrying that Lucy was sitting downstairs all on her own. The ties of motherhood never waned.

Chapter 19

Sophie and Rachel were playing cards on the bedside table. Rachel was smiling, she was starting to remember things, little things, but Sophie was filling her in on anything she wanted to know or anything she couldn't remember fully. Like, Rachel had lived alone in a flat near Leeds town centre. Her mum and dad had died when she was at college and she had been pretty self-sufficient since then. She had worked in a small clothing boutique – and had spent most of her wages there – she enjoyed going out and she enjoyed bringing guys back for a good shag. Sophie spoke candidly about Rachel's life and at times, Rachel was shocked at some of the things Sophie told her.

Sophie told Rachel about the last time they had been out together, the last night she'd seen Rachel, six months ago. SIX MONTHS! She showed her the selfies they had taken before they'd gone out and a few from the night out. Sophie with Harry, Rachel with the guy she'd met that night. He clearly didn't want his photo taken and had kept a hand in the way or had turned his head. Sophie said how much Rachel had enjoyed trying to get his picture – for posterity.

Harry and Sophie had gone home together and hadn't resurfaced until well into the following week. Sophie giggled,

"The sex is amazing! And he can cook! I can't believe we've been together for six months already."

"I can't believe I can't remember the last six months," Rachel frowned. "Did you see me go home with this guy?" She looked at the phone again and tried to zoom in. She couldn't work out if he looked familiar because she'd been looking at the picture so much, or if she actually remembered him.

"You text me from the kebab shop saying, *'He's arrived – phew!'* So I guess he did."

"And I didn't text you the next morning?"

"No, but –" she looked down at her feet, "I was having too much fun to realise and then, you were looking at your messages but not replying so I thought you'd either hooked up and were getting plenty, like me. Or, you were mad at me for something." Her eyes met Rachel's "I'm sorry I didn't check up on you babes."

"Hey, don't you go apologising." Rachel reprimanded.

Sophie was staying in a Premier Inn close to the hospital. Harry had gone back to Leeds for work but Sophie felt it was important that she stay with her friend, just to be there. She visited every day, filling Rachel in on her life and Rachel telling her all she knew about the crash that could have killed her, but stole her memories instead.

"Must have been really scary."

"I couldn't see to begin with – because of the concussion. Now *that* was scary."

"I'd have freaked out." Sophie laughed.

"I think I did!" Rachel laughed too.

One of the male nurses came to the end of her bed around lunchtime. "Visiting time is over, I'm afraid," he smiled at Sophie.

"It's fine," she stretched. "I could do with finding a clothes shop. Harry wasn't able to take time off to bring me a suitcase." She turned to the nurse, "Is there a bus that will get me into town?"

"Yep, there is a bus every twenty minutes from the stop right outside the main A&E department," he replied wheeling up the trolley to take Rachel's blood pressure and temperature.

Sophie kissed Rachel on the forehead and headed out of the ward.

"You ready for some lunch?" the nurse asked.

"Yeah, famished."

"Getting your appetite back, I see," he recorded his observations on her chart, put them back in the end of the bed and looked up at her. "You really are looking much better."

He placed her tray of food on her table and lifted the lid, "Quiche and new potatoes with broccoli," he smiled. "And, it actually looks good enough to eat, today!" he mused and left Rachel to eat her food.

Rachel felt a weight in the pit of her stomach.

She stared after him. What had he just said? "Good enough to eat?" Why did that make her feel so uneasy? Forehead creased, she started to eat her lunch. But the words kept relaying in her mind. "Good enough to eat." "Good enough to eat." Where had she heard those words before and what significance did they have?

Rachel started to eat, the food was good today and she was glad she'd opted for the hot option. Now that Sophie was spending time at the hospital, Rachel's mind was doing more – even if she wasn't physically active, she was using energy laughing, catching up and talking. Who knew that talking used so much energy? She was sleeping better, not waking up every hour throughout the night to check that she was still in the hospital, that she hadn't lost even more of her life, her cheeks had colour and her heart was less lonely.

"You look good enough to eat," she heard the words inside her head, as if someone had whispered them right into her ear. Then, in one split second, a fork full of food almost at her mouth, her mind reconnected a million dots and she screamed.

She screamed as if her life was in danger.

Screamed with fear.

Screamed because there were no words for what she was feeling.

Screamed at the scene that flashed before her eyes. The scene that she was watching unfolded as if she were a fly on the wall. It happened to her.

She saw the man's face, heard his voice and watched what he did to her as if it was on replay.

Her food was on the floor as Rachel kicked and screamed. Eyes wide and still screaming nurses surrounded her bed and pulled the curtains closed. They bleeped for a doctor, they removed the table and lowered the bed, trying to calm her and talk her down. Nothing was working. A few moments later, the doctor arrived. Rachel was still fighting with the nurses who were trying to restrain her angst; arms flailing as she screamed.

The screams of real horror. And when the doctor took out a needle of sedative to try and help relax her, she screamed more and kicked and cried out until she was falling, falling backwards into the darkness.

***

At 2:00 p.m. Sophie arrived to see the police sitting at the side of Rachel's bed.

"Am I allowed to see her?" she asked the nurse at the nurse's station.

"Of course you are. I think they were waiting for you to come back."

Rachel held out her hand as Sophie came towards her. Sophie saw that she was looking pale and drained, like something traumatic had happened whilst she was away.

"Sophie," she paused, "Can you show these officers the photo of the guy I was with that night at REVs please?"

Sophie looked bemused, but did as Rachel asked.

"He is the guy who raped and drugged me," she pointed at him.

Rachel knew 'rape' was strong word to use when you had invited a guy back with you. But he had had sex with her once, consensually and then he had drugged her. Whilst she was in a state of drug induced ecstasy, he'd made her perform for him and then forced himself on her again and again, even after Rachel had clearly tried to stop him. She remembered the horrors now. A tear escaped and ran down her cheek.

Sophie threw her arms around her friend and burst into tears, "Why didn't I come to check on you?" she wailed.

Rachel sat up, squared her shoulders and wiped the tear away, "Because you thought I would be having as good a time as you," Rachel squeezed her hand. "It's okay, you weren't to know."

The police officer asked Sophie if they could take her phone away to get the photo from it and she agreed without hesitation. She would do anything to help catch that evil excuse for a man, who went around drugging and raping innocent women.

"What I don't understand," Sophie started, "Is why he felt he needed to drug you. You are always up for a good night in the sack, you don't need drugging for that."

"Maybe it was about where he took me after that because I don't know what happened, I can't remember anything else yet." Rachel mused. "I think I'd better be prepared to start remembering things," she paused, "Not very nice things either."

"It sounds horrific to say it out loud," Sophie added. "But I hope you do remember," she lowered her gaze, not wishing the painful memories on her friend, but knowing it was inevitable.

"Me too."

Chapter 20

The sun streamed through the rotating doors at the hospital entrance, but today it was Rachel's exit. She had finally been discharged and would only need to return as an outpatient. She walked steadily with her stick, everyday proving easier, with a smile on her face. To make things easier for her appointments, she was renting a small flat a couple of miles from the hospital and Sophie and Harry had already made a start on moving her in; Sophie had brought a suitcase of clothes for her, which were now hanging in the wardrobe, because Rachel didn't have any clothes of her own. When the rent on her flat in Leeds hadn't been paid and the landlady couldn't get hold of Rachel, who had disappeared off the face of the Earth, the landlady had emptied the flat and re-let it. Rachel couldn't complain; she would have done the same. Most people would be gutted, but she wasn't. Losing her memories meant also losing her attachment to 'things.'

The new flat was let fully furnished, which was a bonus. And since Rachel had regained her identity, she'd been able to contact the bank and arrange for new bank cards. She wouldn't be able to work for a while, but she had enough if she dipped into the money her parents had left in trust for her with the intention that she would receive it on her 21st birthday. Because of everything that had happened she had decided to release a small percentage of it early, it only took a few phone calls and some legal paperwork to arrange and it would help get her by until she was back on her feet.

Once Rachel had given her new home the once over, and thanked Sophie and Harry for getting it organised for her, they went shopping to fill the cupboards with food and to get the adult essentials: dusters and polish, toilet rolls, bleach, washing powder.

Sophie added a bottle of prosecco in the trolley to toast Rachel's new life. She was hoping that Rachel would decide to move back to Leeds but after such a horrible trauma, she hadn't made up her mind just yet. The man who had attacked her could be local for all they knew and Rachel couldn't face that just yet.

Walking around the supermarket, they laughed about how bad Rachel's cooking skills were and at the fact that she would be living on ready meals and alcohol.

"Oh, I don't think I'll be drinking much," she spoke openly.

Sophie visibly paused for a moment before catching up, "What're you talking about?"

"Well, I just lost six months of my life. I was pissed when that all started and then drugged. So, I think I'm going to keep a clear head for a while."

Although Sophie's jaw dropped at the statement, she couldn't argue with her.

"Should I put the bubbles back then?"

"I didn't say you couldn't drink," Rachel laughed as Sophie released a breath and relaxed.

They'd bought food for the evening, which Harry cooked. Sophie was right, he was a great chef! They watched a Mamma Mia on TV (much to Harry's disgruntlement - although Rachel was sure she saw him tapping his foot during a couple of the songs). Sophie and Harry stayed the night to make sure Rachel was okay and headed home the following morning, leaving Rachel to settle in, relax and make the flat feel like her home.

"Keep in touch," Sophie kissed her best friend on the cheek. "And if you don't reply to me within twenty minutes, I'll be catching the next train over here to check you are alright!"

"I'll be fine," she winked, "If I don't know who I am, no one else will either. I'm perfectly safe here."

"Don't even joke about it!" Sophie wailed as she climbed into the car and wound the window down.

"Love ya!"

"See you soon!"

Rachel stood at the side of the pavement until the car rounded the corner. She smiled, she couldn't remember much of her past, but she was ready to make a go of her future.

***

Sophie and Harry visited a month later and were impressed to see how well Rachel had settled in to her new life. Sophie wasn't surprised that she'd already found a job in one of the local boutiques and was doing well. She'd stuck to her no drink rule and seemingly wasn't missing her wild life. She looked radiant in her red polo neck jumper and denim skirt and boots, her curls framed her face and she was genuinely smiling.

"You look lovely," Sophie admired and thought inwardly mused, I don't think I'd be anywhere near as strong as her and after everything she's been through.

They hugged, "Yeah, I am taking you both out for dinner."

"Nice, do we need to get dressed for dinner?" Sophie worried.

"Nope, good ol' fashioned pub-grub," she smiled, "Comfy clothes are fine!"

"Great, I'm almost ready for food after that drive." Sophie took off her coat and hung it up on the corner of Rachel's living room door. "So, tell me about the job," she took off her heals and curled her legs underneath her on the sofa.

"I saw the advert in the window when I was walking down to the Oxfam." She saw the look in Sophie's face. "What?"

"A charity shop?" Sophie wrinkled her nose.

"Sophie, I don't have a lot of money and I'm not about to just spend it willy-nilly."

"Yeah but… Have you had a total personality transplant? Who even are you?" she laughed aloud.

"You've got to try it Sophie, it's amazing the things they have – real vintage stuff."

"Vintage? Or do you mean -" she paused "Old?"

Rachel laughed. Sophie laughed.

"Look, I'm just being careful with money. I don't know how long I am going to be living here and I want to be comfortable, that's all."

"I know," Sophie put her hands out to hold Rachel's, "It's just, well - you've changed a bit." Rachel raised her eyebrows. "Oh, no, no. I didn't mean it in a bad way. You've been through a hell of a lot of trauma. You don't remember the things that made you the Rachel I know, knew?" she bit her lip. "You're just different to how you were before and I am still adjusting."

Rachel smiled. Sophie flushed.

Harry wandered in from the kitchen, "Have we got a time for dinner?"

"We can go whenever, I know the landlord, he'll find us a table even if it's booked up," she smiled at them. She felt proud that she was making friends here. She knew she needed to tell Sophie that she was intending to stay in Lancashire. What it lacked in hustle and bustle (compared to Leeds), it made up for it with beautiful scenery and her feelings of safety; being far enough away from Leeds and that man. In fact, she had just agreed a more permanent contract with her landlord. Things were starting to look up for her. She would tell Sophie, she would.

They grabbed their coats and Rachel, her stick as they headed out to the pub at the end of the road.

"Evening Tom," Rachel smiled as she walked towards the bar.

"Hey Rachel," he nodded at Sophie and Harry, "Friends?"

"Yeah, from Leeds."

"Nice, never been to Leeds. Good night life?"

"The best!" Sophie laughed and then fell silent. It might have been the best for her, but it had been the worst for Rachel. She blushed and lowered her head.

Rachel didn't flinch at the comment, she knew Sophie didn't mean it and besides, she'd resolved to leave the past in the past. "Have you got a table for three?" she asked him.

"Sure do. Anything for you," he smiled at her and picked up some menus indicating for the trio to follow him.

Sophie nudged Rachel in the ribs, "He likes you!"

Rachel smiled but said nothing; she knew he did.

While they were waiting for their food to be delivered, Rachel made her little announcement. "I've made a decision." She took a deep breath, "I won't be moving back to Leeds."

As predicted Sophie looked cross. She took a sharp intake of breath before she pouted and slammed her hand down on the table. "When did you decide this?" she tried to hide the disappointment from her voice. Harry reached for Sophie's hand to calm her.

"I can't be in Leeds after everything that happened. I would always be looking over my shoulder Sophie." She pleaded with her eyes. "I wouldn't ever be able to live my life."

"But -" Sophie paused. "What about me?"

"Oh Sophie, you are always welcome here. I'll still be your friend." She took a sip of her drink. "Please understand. This is what is best for me."

Rachel didn't speak, instead she let Sophie mull things over in her mind.

Instead, it was Harry spoke up, "I think you've been very brave," he smiled. "After everything you've been through. You've got a job; you haven't let it ruin your life. You're doing amazing. Honestly." Noticing Sophie's face, he smiled, "What? I haven't known Rachel for that long, well not properly anyway, and I am so proud of what I've seen her manage to overcome."

Sophie stopped picking at the bar mat and looked up at Harry, he wasn't usually a talker and at this spiel her jaw had dropped. Harry looked at her and continued, "She's done really well. I knew a girl who got beaten up on her way home to halls one night and she never left the dorm again. She was a wreck." He nodded towards Rachel, "Your best friend is a force to be reckoned with and I think she is making the right decision."

Rachel beamed. He was right. Even she hadn't given herself that much credit. She was a fighter, yes, but he made her feel proud of how far she had come. "Thanks Harry."

He nodded.

"Yeah, okay." Sophie agreed. "But we still have to do stuff together. I can't agree to a best friend relationship just via text and video calls." She took a large sip of her gin. "I'll have to find someone else if it gets too boring."

This made Rachel laugh. "As if," she laughed. "You won't find anyone more interesting than me."

They enjoyed their night and the next few days and when Sophie and Harry had left, Rachel sat on the sofa. Was she really that different to the person she was before? After pondering the alternative version of herself, she decided that she liked the person that she was now and that whoever or whatever she had been like before, it didn't matter. She was happy now. That was all that mattered.

***

Three months on and life was great, she'd been seeing Tom, casually. She'd had no further flashbacks into her missing six months and the doctors assured her that if she wanted help to remember, they could arrange for psychological support which could help, but there were no guarantees. She'd decided against it. She told Sophie on the phone one night.

"Well, it's your decision at the end of the day." Sophie remarked. She'd played devil's advocate to be sure that Rachel had thought through all of the options available to her. "We can probably agree that what happened can't have been that good, and why would you want to remember the bad stuff when you are about to move onto a new relationship?"

"Exactly." Rachel smiled, she had hoped Sophie would agree with her.

She and Tom had started to date officially. It was nice to have someone pay her compliments. He was twelve years older than her and at thirty two he was admittedly looking for more than a fling. He knew about her amnesia and the events that had brought her here from Leeds and he didn't pressure her to move their relationship onto a physical one quicker than she was ready. They hadn't slept together yet, but that wasn't everything, was it?

In the June of 2018, three months after they started spending more time together; a whole year after the accident and 18 months since her night of horror in Leeds, Rachel determined to take the next steps in her relationship with

Tom. She deserved to be truly happy. She'd suffered enough and the amnesia was a constant reminder of the lost months of her life, it needed replacing with happy memories. She messaged Tom one evening on her way home from work.

Food at mine tonight?

His response was immediate, Sounds good.

Want to sleep over?

…

Those bloody dots. He was clearly writing and rewording a message. Fear gripped at her stomach, what if he didn't want to sleep with her? They hadn't talked about it that much. Maybe once?

I'd love to, if you'll have me.

She breathed a sigh of relief.

I'm ready for this xx

She put her phone into her bag, almost bumping in a man on the narrow alleyway as she did so.

"Sorry," she smiled, "I was miles away." She tried to side step him, but they both went the same way and then they both went the other way. He was looking at her as if she should know who he was, "Well, this is awkward," she flustered, looking at his face.

Rachel stopped trying to side step him and waited for him to go around her. But he didn't. How odd. He was still staring at her and his eyes were growing smaller as he furrowed his brow. His nose flared and in an instant, his face was wretched. She felt scared.

"Awkward? I'll tell you what is awkward," he spat the words in her face. "Awkward is bumping into the girl whose boyfriend killed your son."

"Err, what?" Rachel was genuinely confused.

It took her until the split second before his fist made contact with her jaw to connect the dots. The accident. The car crash that had been the start of her current life. She still didn't know how she had gotten to be in that car, but she knew that the driver had killed a boy before being killed himself in the collision that followed.

Rachel stumbled backwards, suddenly realising how precarious her situation was. She scrambled in her bag for her phone but whilst her concentration was elsewhere, he punched her again. This time in the ribs and then he swiped her legs from underneath her. She fell in a crumpled heap on the ground. He rolled her over and sat on her.

In that spit second several things happened at once.

Rachel had a flashback. She was on a bed; a man on top of her forcing something into her mouth. At the same time as the flashback, which temporarily incapacitated her, this man started punching her face, over and over relentless, determined. Rachel looked into her attacker's eyes and saw nothing but pure hatred.

With the next punch, something inside her brain snapped and the sea of once-lost memories flooded her mind; rape, prostitution, drugs, beatings, being sold for sex and suddenly, finally, the reason for this; the face of the little boy as the car slammed into him. As her eyes started to close and the world around her dim, she realised that the anticipation of dying was far worse than the event itself.

Chapter 21

Alex was driving back from his weekly shop at the supermarket, his least favourite chore, when he saw an ambulance and police cars blocking the road up ahead. The traffic had been stopped and there was quite a police presence. They were milling around the street talking to pedestrians and walking in and out of the shop on the corner. There was a tape boundary across the alleyway and a tent was being erected.

As it was a warm evening, he allowed the windows to wind down completely before he turned off his engine, this better not take long. He had frozen food in the boot and it wouldn't take them long to defrost in this heat. Pedestrians were being dispersed by the police officers and they wandered lazily up the road, looking over their shoulders as they did, hoping to hear something and find out more.

Alex overheard snippets of conversations as pedestrians crossed the road around the car:

"Beaten to death."

"Arrested at the scene."

"Monster."

"All captured on CCTV."

"Face smashed in. Unrecognisable."

"Poor girl."

"Masses of curly black hair was all I saw of her before the police move me on."

All of a sudden, Alex's blood ran cold. He jumped out the car and ran. Ran as fast as he could to where the police were and then pushed his way past, ducked under the unsuspecting officers to get closer to where the paramedics and police officers had created a barrier halfway down the alleyway. Beyond them, the body of a woman clearly dead, black curls splayed out in a pool of red blood.

"Please God, NO!" he screamed.

He fell to his knees and screamed. Then stood up again and stumbled forward. This has happened too many times his heart broke. Now she was dead he wept. That bastard had finally killed the one girl he had ever loved.

A police officer came up to him. "Are you okay sir?" Alex lifted his face and recognised the officer. She recognised him too and questioned, "Alex?"

He nodded, "He's killed her this time, hasn't he? Please tell me I'm wrong." He looked up and pleaded with the kind police officer. He had met this officer on several throughout the investigation into Lucy's attacks and her eyes were full of sorrow.

The police officer was trying to get Alex's attention. "Alex?" She crouched down on the ground next to him. "Alex, this isn't Lucy."

With sudden clarity, he stopped crying, "It isn't?"

"No." She helped him to his feet and looked over to her shoulder to her colleague to indicate that she had this under control. "I thought it was too when I got here, but we've checked and Lucy is at home with her mother and one of our officers."

"But...?" seeing the body lying there, the hair and the blood, it was hard not to see Lucy, the girl on the floor looked identical in every way that he could see.

"It's possible that someone thought it was Lucy. In which case, be thankful that Lucy is at home."

"Did he get away?"

"Not this time. I can't go into details. More than my job's worth, but safe to say that Lucy will be much safer with him behind bars."

***

Two hours later, Alex sat in the police station waiting for his boss, Pete, to meet him. Alex needn't have come but he wanted to be there when Pete identified the man in custody to be the man from Astra-Tech. Alex had considered calling Sharon to let her know. But they were divorced now and he really didn't want to have to go through the whole palaver of breaking contact again.

Pete arrived about 25 minutes after Alex.

"Hey man," he sat on the chair next to Alex. "You look white as a ghost. You ok?"

"Not okay, Pete." Alex managed to get the words out although he was close to tears. The day's events and the fact that this man may have intended to kill Lucy - that this poor girl had gotten in the way - was causing him immense pain.

"What's happened? Is Lucy okay?"

"Thankfully yes," he took a deep breath and stood up, pacing the area in front of the desk trying to get the duty officers attention. "But the girl who looked almost identical isn't okay."

"He beat someone else by mistake?"

"Beat up? Try, killed. Intentionally."

Saying it out loud was too much for Alex. The air inside the police station was stifling and he made a dash out of the doors to throw up at the side of the building. Pete was close behind him.

"You saw?"

"I saw enough to think it was her and know she was dead."

"Ah, shit Alex, I'm sorry. Have you spoken to Lucy?"

"No answer. But there is an officer with her."

Alex took a few deep breaths and a swill of water to clear his mouth and then headed inside where the duty officer was now back behind the desk.

Pete went over to make his arrival known. "Peter O'Neil, I am here to help with the identification of a suspect."

A few minutes later, Pete was looking through a series of photographs. "Nope, none of these are photographs of Jon Ferguson," he told the officer

"None?" the officer clarified.

"None of them. I'm 100% sure. I met him five times in total during the project. There is no photo of him here." He handed the photograph back to the police officer.

"In that case, we can assume that this Jon isn't involved."

Back in the station's reception area, Pete told Alex.

"You were sure?"

Pete nodded.

Alex should have been relieved. But there was another emotion rearing its ugly head. Resentment. Suddenly he was angry that he had been implicated in any of this. He had broken it off with Lucy for her own safety when actually she was never in any danger because of him. He had missed out on spending time with her and valuable time at that. She could have been killed today had she been in the wrong place and without him too. It didn't bear thinking about. He walked out of the station without saying goodbye and headed straight for his car.

***

Lucy had just returned from a photo identification appointment at the police station where she had identified a man as her attacker. Now, sitting in her mum's kitchen, the family liaison officer hovering in the doorway, she was aware of her phone vibrating on the table across from her as she spoke to the police officer who had just arrived. She'd had to sit down.

"Dead?" she questioned.

"Yes."

"And you think that he might have been after me? That this poor girl who looked like me was killed by mistake?"

"It's something that we are looking into."

She felt the blood drain from her face. Her mum was crying at the kitchen sink. Partly in relief but also in guilt that she was relieved someone else's daughter had been killed in her daughter's stead. How cruel this world was that she was grateful someone had been murdered in cold blood.

"And he will be staying in custody?" Lucy needed to know that she was safe to leave the house without the fear of being killed.

"Absolutely," he reassured her. "Not a judge in the land would grant him his freedom after today."

The officer's radio crackled into life and he left the room to talk in private. Lucy put her head in her hands, her mind racing.

A few moments later the officer returned, "We've had another update." He sat down at the table.

***

The drive to Maggie's house seemed to take forever even though there was no traffic. Once there, he ran across the pebbled driveway to Maggie who was already opening the door for him. Her arms were around Alex and she was apologising through the tears.

"I'm so sorry I ever thought any of this could be because of you. I was just so -"

"It's okay Maggie," he hugged her briefly, impatient to see Lucy. "Is Lucy inside?"

"Yes, in the kitchen," she waved her hand in the general direction, even though he knew where it was.

"May I?"

"Of course."

He ran past her and through the lounge into the kitchen where Lucy was sat opposite an officer, she had clearly been crying.

"Alex," she wept, getting up from the seat and finding security in the warmth and firmness of his body as he held her close.

She cried. He held her.

"I'll leave you to your evening," the officer stood to leave, beckoning the family liaison officer to follow him outside for a moment.

"Thank you," Alex nodded his appreciation and returned his head to resting on Lucy's.

Chapter 22

There was still a lot to talk about but for now, Alex was feeling way better than he had in weeks. He stayed at Maggie's with Lucy that night. There was only had a single bed in Lucy's room so they had slept on the sofa; him sat up, her snuggled into the crook of his arm. They watched TV until late into the night, neither of them focussing on any program but also, neither of them ready to sleep; the adrenaline of the day still coursing through their veins. When she eventually fell asleep, he couldn't. The smell of her hair, the weight of her body leaning against him, it just felt so overwhelmingly right that he spent most of the night just appreciating her being there, making up for the weeks he hadn't been there for her.

As the sun rose, he let her sleep and he wandered into the kitchen, made a coffee and then sat on the garden wall looking out over the fields. The weather this summer was ridiculous, like living abroad. He ran over all the events of the previous day in his head and again, a lump in his throat was so grateful that it hadn't been Lucy lay in that pool of blood.

He heard a noise behind him and Lucy joined him. "I'm going to go to bed, I have a crick in my neck from sleeping on you," she smiled up at him.

He kissed her forehead and they hugged.

"I still have questions for you though, Alex," she looked up at him. "About that guy, and his wife."

His face fell but he accepted that she would want answers. "I will tell you everything and answer any questions you ask, but for now, go get some sleep." She tiptoed and kissed him on the lips. The electricity that passed through them made both of them smile as she walked back into the house.

"Sleep well," he called after her.

"I won't have a choice, I doubt an explosion would wake me, I'm *that* tired." she looked over her shoulder at him. Damn she was sexy without even trying.

He headed back in and despite the caffeine, once he lay down on the sofa, he fell asleep.

***

The smell of bacon woke him, his nose alert yet his body exhausted. He opened his eyes and remembered where he was, his mind having had actually switched off and allowed him to rest. He was aware of voices and moved his eyes to find the source. The news was on, volume low and as his eyes scanned more of the room, he saw Lucy sitting, cross legged in the arm chair.

"Mum," she whisper-shouted into the kitchen.

Maggie walked in, tea-towel in her hand. Lucy nodded at the TV. There was a picture of a beautiful girl, pale skin, green eyes and freckles. But what stood out the most was her tousled black, curly hair. "She looks so like you, poor girl."

"I still want to know what it is about me," Lucy sounded justifiably sad. "What have I done to him to make him want to kill me?"

Alex was awake now and listening to the news report.

A 39 year old man has been held to assist with enquiries after a woman was beaten to death in the centre of Blackburn yesterday in a vicious and unprovoked attack. Rachel Carnegie had left work and was walking on her usual route home when she was approached by a man who punched her repeatedly in the face.

Police are appealing to anyone who saw the attack or anyone acting suspiciously at any point yesterday to come forward. Any drivers are being urged to check their dash-cam footage and police are reviewing CCTV footage in the area.

Our thoughts are with the friends and relatives at this time.

The cameras showed the scene of the incident which was filling up with flowers and people were filmed talking about their shock that something like this could happen here. They talked about how she was a lovely girl who had only lived here a short while and that she was always friendly when people saw her in the shop.

Alex mused, *people rarely have horrible things to say about the dead.*

Lucy had been told that the man who had attacked her was Michael Simpson and she was now googling him, checking his profile on Facebook (there was a local profile without a photo so Lucy assumed that was his, and she tried to find him on Instagram (he wasn't on there) she was desperate to find out what their connection was and why he hated her so much.

"Ah, Alex, you're awake." Maggie noted, "Would you like a bacon buttie and a cup of coffee?"

"That would be great," he smiled at her. She was always looking after her guests, always the hostess.

Lucy looked up as Alex turned himself around so that he was sitting on the sofa instead of lying down. She stood up, blanket around her shoulders, and came to sit next to him. As she rested her head on his shoulder, she showed him the profile of the man she suspected was Michael Simpson.

"Why does this man hate me so much?"

He took her phone and started to scroll through the profile. There wasn't much there, a photo of him and his wife on their wedding day was the only photograph, there were no personal posts just shares of other posts. The most recent post was from a little over a year ago. It was a simple picture of a blue heart. There were over a hundred comments and he clicked to view them all.

Sorry for your loss.

We are devastated for you and Megan.

Sending love.

Cannot believe this has happened.

Devastating news, our hearts are with you at this time.

All the comments were in a similar vain. Alex came out of Facebook and opened Lucy's internet. He typed in Michael Simpson Lancashire, 2017. A stream of search results flooded the phone screen and Alex clicked on the first one.

Police have released the name of the boy who was mown down by a reckless driver on Wednesday as 7 year old Thomas Michael Simpson. Thomas was on his way home from football practice on Wednesday 14th June when a car, travelling at over 40 mph ploughed into him as he was crossing the road. Family and friends say that he was the kindest, most loving boy they knew and that this loss will be felt forever. His mother, Megan Simpson and father, Michael Simpson have asked that their privacy is observed at this time. The funeral will be held at St Christopher's on Sunday 25th June at 10 a.m.

Alex came back to the search page and selected another article, reading it aloud.

"Police have released the name of the driver of the black KIA that killed 7 year old Thomas on Wednesday 14th June. Thomas had been on his way home from football practice with his mum when the car, driven by Muhammed Azim Khan, ploughed into

him. Thomas died from his injuries on the way to hospital. The passenger, an unnamed female, survived the impact and was also taken to hospital."

Maggie brought in a plate with a bacon buttie and a mug of steaming hot tea. Alex read another article through bites of bacon.

"The father of Thomas Simpson, the 7 year old boy killed last month on 14th June has offered a reward for any information relating to the man and woman who were in the car that killed his son. Michael Simpson has offered £500 to anyone who has information regarding the couple, one of whom died in the crash. Mr Simpson was heard to say, "She is alive and my son is not, the least she can do is tell me why."

He paused and looked at Lucy, "It would appear that he is a grieving man who wants answers."

She nodded.

"But what has any of this got to do with me?"

"I don't know. But I am actually beginning to wonder if it ever did."

"That poor girl though." Big fat tears started to run down Lucy's face and Alex instinctively pulled her close and held her sobbing, shaking frame, stroking her hair until she calmed.

Later in the afternoon, Alex broached the topic of going home, together.

213

"The place feels empty without you and I'm," he paused, "I've – I can't not have you in my life."

"I need to know about this woman. The one you slept with." She looked up and met his eyes, "The police said it was early last year." Her voice dropped to a barely audible whisper, "That's when we first got together."

He closed his eyes and sucked in a deep breath.

"You know the very first day that we met? When I made you spill your coffee?"

She nodded.

"I was supposed to be meeting Sharon at a hotel." He looked at the floor and picked at a piece of fluff with his sock. "I'd already decided that this would be the last time. She was nice, but I wasn't ready for anything as full on as she was." He looked at Lucy, who was listening intently. "I didn't end up going." Another deep breath. "After I said goodbye to you, I went home."

Lucy raised her eyebrows. "Is that it?"

"Yeah. I went on holiday with the lads – climbing in Font. Didn't even take my phone with me. When I got home, she'd left a ton of messages, really pissed off, then really sorry, then really angry and tearful. It wasn't fun." He chanced a look at Lucy who was now looking out of the window. "About a week after I got back, I came to the coffee shop and you were there." He exhaled.

"Guess you got lucky-ish with me then," she smiled.

"What do you mean 'ish'?" he used his fingers to quote the 'ish.'

"Well, I am much easier going, don't demand much… But, you know, I get beat up quite a bit."

She'd said it as a joke, but Alex's heart broke for her and he pulled her into an embrace so genuinely protective of her that she melted into his strong arms and then the tears came.

"Lucy, I fell in love with you the second I saw you." He pulled her away and kissed her nose. "I kept falling in love with you every single time I saw you after that. And I want to spend the rest of my life with you – if you'll still have me?"

She wiped her eyes with her sleeves.

"I do," she smiled before she resumed her place in the crook of his arm. "And I want to come home."

Alex beamed, eyes threatening tears, he held her close.

Chapter 23

Michael sat opposite the two police officers and next to the duty solicitor. He was advised that they had CCTV of the incident in the alleyway. He didn't deny anything.

"What was the reason for your attack on this girl?" asked the male officer.

"She was involved in the crash that killed my son Thomas." The officers shared a sideways glance.

"When was this accident?"

"June 2017," he paused, "Black KIA ploughed into my Thomas on the street in broad daylight. He died from his injuries," Michael was barely holding it together, shoulders trembling and his face showing the depth of his pain. "The driver Azim Khan was killed in the crash." His lip curled in hatred, "He deserved it – so did she."

"So in your eyes, this was a justified action?"

"Yes. And I'd do it again."

Michael's solicitor put her arm on his elbow and leant in to whisper something in his ear but he shook the arm away.

The male officer spoke up next.

"Mr Simpson, as you have admitted that you killed a person intentionally and have shown no remorse. I have no option but to charge you with the murder of Rachel Carnegie."

He lowered his head. "We also have CCTV footage to indicate that you were the perpetrator in a number of other attacks on a young girl, in a supermarket and on the high street in town."

There was no denial.

"Therefore you are also charged with three accounts of grievous bodily harm to a Miss Lucy Lawrence."

"I don't know no Lucy Lawrence."

The police officer showed him an image from the CCTV on the date he had attacked the girl who had come out from the wedding dress shop. A different girl. He'd messed up. Had he even killed the right one? He started to panic and then, the weight of his actions tumbled down on him and he paled. He tried to voice his thoughts, but stammered and stuttered, clearly feeling that he was being unfairly punished. Finally, he shouted out, "She killed my son, she owed me. A life for a life."

"Mr Simpson, you cannot simply take a situation like that into your own hands. There were investigations into the accident that killed your son and Miss Carnegie was not considered to be guilty in any way."

The solicitor asked for a moment with her client and so the officer switched off the tape and left the room.

Through the glass, the officers could see Michael break, he wept, banged his head on the table in visible distress.

Inside the room, Michael was indeed stressed about the situation. He stood by his words, he would do it all over again. He did it for Thomas. He did it for Megan, so that she would know that everyone who had been involved in Thomas' death had been punished with death. Now, what scared him the most, terrified him in fact, was that now that he was here, they would not let him go – what would happen to Megan? Her mental state was so delicate and she relied on him mentally and physically for everything. Now that he was not there for her, who would care for her? He needed to speak to her but he knew that she would not answer the phone. This distressed him more than any other situation he had ever been in. Megan would be lost without him. She would think that he abandoned her and only God knew what her fragile mind would do, how she would cope. He asked the duty solicitor to pass a message onto his wife if she could. He was sorry, he'd made sure the debt had been repaid, but he now had to pay the price.

The police officers came back and took Michael into another room for photographing, fingerprinting and the logging of all his personal belongings. Then he was taken to a small cell where he would wait for transport to a bigger, more permanent custody suite to await the long process of sentencing.

***

Since Azim had left with Rachel, life had been a little rougher on Jen. As much as she had relied on him to get her work, it wasn't that hard to find her own source of income – it just took longer and more walking in ridiculous heals. Walking the streets at night and avoiding the cops wasn't as easy as being handed guys with cash on a plate. However, at least this way, she got to keep all of her earnings; that was something at least. She managed. The girls all still lived in the flats, the electricity had been switched off when the bills hadn't been paid, but there was shelter from the elements and as yet, the weather had been unusually warm.

She was walking her usual streets one evening when she caught sight of the headline of a newspaper being read in the night café. The headline was eye catching enough to draw her eye, but it was the picture that made her inhale sharply.

DAYLIGHT MURDER

Without a second thought she walked into the café and sat down so that she could see the paper. She couldn't read the article, but the woman on the front cover was definitely Rachel. She would recognise that face and those curls anywhere.

When Azim hadn't returned, she'd hoped something bad had happened to him and that Rachel had gotten out and free.

It seemed as if she had, but that death had found her anyway. Murdered though? Who would want to do that? Had Azim done it? Had she run away and he'd gone after her that night? Maybe one of her ex-clients? Jen wondered if she would be able to help the investigations, and whether she should go to the police.

"Can I get you a drink?" the woman behind the counter was staring at Jen in an 'order something or leave' sort of way.

"Yes, please. Coffee, two sugars." She walked up to the counter to pay and spotted another copy of the newspaper on another table. She picked it up to read. Skimming it, she found the key facts.

Tragedy, man arrested.

No need to go to the police then, probably for the best.

***

Lucy had agreed to go back home with Alex and she had to admit, the place had missed her. The dishes on the drainer were bone dry and she wondered if Alex had even bothered with putting them in the cupboard before using them again. The floor hadn't been swept, the flowers in the vase were drooping beyond any magic she could work on them and the mat by the back door was squint – somehow that bothered her more than the other things in the kitchen. She held her breath and walked into the lounge where she counted no less than five mugs, three glasses and a plate lying around. There was dust on the mantelpiece and the curtains, although opened, had not been tied back – yet.

"I'll bet you a fiver that the bed isn't made and the bath isn't rinsed," she raised a finger at Alex and waggled it. Instead of protesting, he went straight to his wallet and pulled out a fiver for her. She laughed and nudged him. "Well, I think that you should cook me dinner whilst I tackle the house," she smiled and headed towards the cupboard behind the kitchen door for polish and a duster.

Later that evening, after an hour and a half of cleaning, and a steaming hot shower Lucy cosied herself in comfy slippers and fluffy dressing gown and found Alex in the kitchen looking for inspiration for dinner.

"What do you fancy?" he was asking as she walked in and leant on the kitchen counter. She was hungry, but for something else.

"Well there is something that I like a lot that I've not had for a little while," she was smiling at her own provocativeness before he even realised what she was talking about.

"Oh really? What would that be?" he didn't look at her and pretended not to notice the alluring tone to her voice.

He heard her move closer and held his breath, every hair on his body tingling in anticipation of her touch. She walked up behind him and placed her arms around his waist, just low enough to cause him to exhale, and she rested her head on his shoulders. "Well, I haven't had any male attention for such a long time -" she breathed. "I might have forgotten what to do," she held back a giggle at how girlish she sounded.

"I don't think so," he whispered as he rearranged himself inside his jeans.

Suddenly the time that had forced them to be apart needed to be caught up and replaced by closeness. She found his jeans buttons, tugging at them and then pushing her fingers inside. His breathing was heavy as he realised he needed the same closeness. He had almost lost her again and he needed to be physically connected to her. He turned around to face her and untied her dressing gown, noticing that she was wearing nothing underneath, he let it hang loosely at her sides. She was beautiful, his eyes paused for a moment over her breasts before taking in her full length. She stepped forward and lifted his t-shirt up and over his head. Once his chest was exposed, she ran her nails across his abdomen and took pride in his reaction. He lifted her up and sat her on the counter, kissing her urgently, passionately.

He kissed her breasts, her stomach, between her legs and when she leant back, inviting him closer, he did not hesitate, if she wanted him right here, she would get him, right here. He pulled his jeans and boxers down over his hips and let them fall to the floor and picking her up just enough he lowered her onto him. Lucy used the kitchen counter to support her as he shuddered in ecstasy and then they found their momentum. Her bracing against the kitchen counter and him thrusting deep inside her. He came quickly calling out her name and she held him. Not ready for it to be over, she led him into the living room and sat on the arm of the sofa and with a glint in her eye, she pulled him towards her and then pushed him down into a kneeling position. She wanted to come too, but she wanted his mouth to do it.

He did as she wanted, following her body language and as her body trembled in pleasure, he carried her to the bedroom where they made love.

"Do you still want to marry me, Lucy?" he asked as she lay in his arms afterwards.

"Will I get to have sex with you, like this, forever?"

He smiled, "You will."

She rolled over towards him, hooking one leg over his, "And will you always put me first and treat me like a princess?"

"Absolutely," he squeezed her tight.

"Then, I guess-" her stomach growled. "Hmm – I think I need to make this decision on a full stomach." She winked at him.

"Very sensible," he grabbed his phone from the side, "But I am not leaving this bed unless it is to answer the door to a takeaway!"

They ordered food and made love once more. Enjoying the reconnection and the sex they'd both missed so much.

The food arrived, and they enjoyed catching up in each other's company. Allowing bygones and misunderstandings to fade into insignificance.

Once Lucy had eaten her fill, she smiled at Alex. "I will."

He looked at her, confused momentarily and then, realising that she was answering his question, beamed at her and kissed her once again. Things were definitely back on track. Life was good. Lucy was well and they were getting married.

Chapter 24

The months rolled by and were filled with wedding planning, the big day was not far away now. Lucy's dress was steamed and hanging up at the bridal shop as was her veil, ready to be picked up and taken to the hotel the night before the wedding. She had booked her makeup artist and hairdresser. Alex's tux (yes he wanted to wear a tuxedo) was hanging in the cupboard in the bedroom and Lucy had thoroughly enjoyed help him try it on. He looked hot in it and she'd had to stop herself from pouncing on him, "You'll get it creased," he had pushed her away so that he could remove it in peace. "It fits fine, I won't need to try it on every week," he winked and she'd moaned in protest.

Everything was falling into place.

Michael, the man who had attacked her had been charged and was being held on a custodial sentence. Lucy, Alex and Maggie had been in attendance at court when he had confirmed his identity and pled guilty to two of Lucy's attacks and the murder of Rachel. He had pled not-guilty to attempted murder in Lucy's first attack. He had told the court that he had made a mistake attacking Lucy, that Rachel was his intended victim.

Lucy realised how lucky she had been to still be living at her mum's during that time and not out and about. The possibility of her being killed in a case of mistaken identity was too big a concept to hold in her head and she had started to feel sick and dizzy at the thought of it.

"I need some air," she whispered to Alex as she stood up and headed to the door. Barely through them, had she broken into a run towards the ladies loos where she vomited. Sitting on the cold tile floor, she calmed her breathing until she heard her mum coming in after her.

"All a bit much lovely?" Maggie had asked.

"Yeah," Lucy managed to stand up.

Maggie continued, "He'll get what he deserves, Lucy."

Lucy nodded and gave her mum a hug.

Back out in the lobby, Alex was waiting for them, "He's being remanded in custody until the trial."

The three of them, Lucy in the middle left the court building. Glad to have closed that chapter of their lives.

Lucy's life continued in blissful happiness. Wedding preparations took over her thoughts and between work, phone calls to florists, venues, meal tastings and final dress fitting, Lucy was living in her perfect bubble. Not a care in the world.

***

With just five weeks until the wedding, Lucy was getting ready for her 'hen' day with friends from school. Penny hadn't told her where they were going, but if Penny had picked it, Lucy knew that she was going to have the best day. She slipped into her green wrap dress and adjusted the neckline. She tied her hair up and smiled in the mirror. Ready.

Penny did her proud! Spa day with afternoon tea and treatments, followed by drinks in town. The sun was streaming in through the windows of the gin bar where they sat. Lucy hadn't stopped smiling all day. The girls had all chipped in with the cost and Lucy hadn't felt this relaxed in ages. It was nice to stop and do something outside school. The new school year had started and Lucy, having had quite a bit of time off work in the last academic year was determined to get through the year intact. It did appear more likely now that the whole mistaken identity palaver was over.

Lucy clinked glasses with Cheryl and Natalie, Penny and Jo. "This has been the best day."

"Here's to the blushing bride!" Jo's voice sang over the others.

Cheryl was enjoying her drinks very much and Lucy feared that she'd still be hungover on Monday morning and Natalie was pretty chatty with the guys at the bar. Everyone was having fun. Penny had her next game ready. Dares. The girls had to pull out a card from the pack and complete the challenge on the back.

Cheryl dived straight in. "I'd better go first before I fall flat on my face and make a tit of myself," she laughed. She pulled out her card and laughed. "Okay, this is ridiculous." Penny grinned, these had been fun to prepare. Thankfully, the one that Lucy would get was hidden in the bottom of Penny's bag.

"What does it say?" Natalie was asking.

"Watch and see." Cheryl took the last swig of her gin. Nodding at Penny, she said, "Time me." She tilted her head back and rested the gin glass on her chin. She couldn't talk from this position but the squeals from the rest of the group at the ridiculous sight made Cheryl start to tremble with mirth until the glass almost fell - she caught it before it did.

"Did I managed - long enough?" she raised an eyebrow at Penny.

Penny turned her phone around. 01:27 "Nope, three seconds off."

"Bugger!"

"Why? Are there penalties?" Natalie asked.

"Yes, my round! Again!" and off Cheryl traipsed to the bar.

The chitter chatter of the girls started up once again until, wondering where Cheryl was, Penny shouted out, "Hey, Cheryl! Are you coming back?" Cheryl looked over her shoulder. She was talking to someone at the bar.

"I'm coming!" She started tottering back over and the guy she had been talking to started to follow her. "Lucy! Do you recognise him? He says he knows you from Uni! Small world eh!?"

Lucy's heart stopped and she sobered up instantly. The instinct to flee tried to overcome her. She had to get out but to save face, she had to play ignorant. If any of her friends spotted the millisecond flash of recognition, they didn't let on – thank you gin – *he* did though. And his eyes were boring into her skull. "I don't think I do," she smiled sweetly shaking her head. "Which University did you attend?" she asked him, keeping up the pretence of ignorance.

"Cumbria."

"Oh, Lancaster for me. You must have the wrong person." And with that she took a rather large sip of her gin and tried to blend back in with her friends and their mindless chatter. His eyes glared at her for a moment longer and then he walked away.

She excused herself to the ladies loos a few minutes later, where she locked herself in the cubicle and sat, terrified on the toilet seat, tears running down her face.

***

2017

An adept pair of fingers typed LUCY COOKE into the google search bar and pressed enter.

Results flashed up on the screen. She's been a witness in a case a few years ago, there were a few articles on that, but nothing recent. Nothing at all. Fists slammed on the table a glass thrown against the wall in rage.

After another hour of internet searches, he came across a site giving details of names changed by deed poll. He found that Lucy Cooke had changed her name to Lucy Lawrence. The dates fitted. This could be her.

He searched for Lucy Lawrence.

Facebook Profile: Lucy Lawrence.

LinkedIn Profile: Lucy Lawrence.

The Meadows Primary School: Lucy Lawrence.

The mouse clicked on the third link and proceeded to find the staff 'Who's Who' scrolling until Lucy's face scrolled into sight.

Yes it was her.

Finding the contact details for the school was next and printing the address.

She would pay for what she did.

Chapter 25

2010

Student nightlife was great! Lucy enjoyed letting her hair down. She'd always been so sensible and well presented, that being able to be the 'wild child' was fun! She ordered another round of shots at the bar and downed two before carrying the other four back to her friends. She had one year left at university and then the sensible life would reconvene.

Lucy worked hard by day and partied hard on student nights when the drinks were cheap, the music cheesy and her dance moves even worse. She didn't care. If life wasn't for living to the full, then what was it all about? One day she would settle down and have her dream job, but for now, she was drunk, wild and happy.

As the terms went by, Lucy's nights out slowly became sponsored by MASTERCARD. She was going to be earning a good wage as a teacher and she would worry about those debts when she needed to. Yet, she considered getting a part time job to help fund her student social life but the hours were too restricting. It wasn't until she saw an advert on the student board that she saw a way that she could earn money whilst still enjoying her life.

Need Extra Cash? Be a paid date, no strings, and no favours. Accompany professional persons to important dinners and earn money in the meantime.

It had taken a few moments to actually take in what the advert was for. Lucy warily eyed the 'no favours' part and wondered if that was a lie! Intrigue got the better of her and she'd written down the number, 'just in case'. On checking her bank balance the next day, the 'just in case,' became a 'needed now' situation and so she'd called the number.

"Hello?" the voice on the other end was a female, older than Lucy, but sounded no older than thirty.

"Err, I'm, I picked up this number from the advert in the student halls. Something about being a paid date?

"Great, tell me about yourself."

"I'm training to be a teacher –"

"Not that stuff, boring Hun, tell me your stats."

"Oh, sorry, size eight."

"Bra size?"

"36B."

"Height?"

"Five-eight."

"Weight?"

"Eight stone, ten."

"What do you drink?"

"Whatever's on offer," Lucy cringed at her own voice on that question.

"Availability?"

"Most evenings if I haven't got an assignment due in."

"Okay. So," there was an audible pause at the other end of the phone and paper rustling.

"What's your name?"

"Lucy."

"Okay Lucy, I have a job tonight if you're free?"

"Oh!"

"Is that okay? £250 cash to join a 47 year old to a golf presentation."

"What do I need to do?"

"Wear a nice dress, smile, meet him before the event at a specified place, arrive with him, make polite conversation with him and then eat and drink and go home with £250."

"Is it that easy?"

"Yes."

On her first 'job' as an escort she had borrowed her friends long silver dress, worn her heeled sandals and her black curls piled up on her head in a high bun. She'd never worn much makeup but felt the need to tonight, almost like a mask. With her face made up, she'd looked in the mirror, the mascara made her lashes long and seductive and – urgh – she'd quickly washed her face and started again. Seductive was *not* the desired look for tonight. She re-did her eyes and added a pale pink blusher and lip gloss - much better, she was set to go. She picked up her clutch, containing just her dorm key fob and headed for the door. That was when the nerves started.

She'd been more nervous about meeting a total stranger for dinner than the actual job itself. But it had been absolutely delightful. A nice meal at a business presentation, a few drinks (she didn't go over board – no one wants to be embarrassed by the pretty hired girl). He was nice guy (reminded her of her grandad, but a little younger) and home and in bed before midnight with £250 in her purse. Easy! She paid the money straight onto her credit card as she'd promised herself she would.

Whenever she had a free evening, she would call the number, speak to the woman, go on a date and get paid. It was ridiculous money for what was in reality, a posh meal, posh wine and great dancing. Instead of going out with the girls and spending money she didn't have, she would go out with sophisticated guys, have the best food, even better wine and go home richer. It was a no brainer. The only problem was, her girlfriends wanted to know why she was ditching them and where she was going. Lucy didn't want to tell them the truth. She was training to be a teacher and that little bit of knowledge in the hands of her lovely, but talkative-when-drunk friends, would not ensure her safe passage into the professional role of primary school teacher. She told them that she'd met a guy, he was older than her she was and promised that if things got serious, she would tell them more.

She attended many events with many good looking guys in her last year at university. Sometimes they flirted, sometimes she accepted more alcohol than was wise, but she always went home alone.

Well. Nearly always.

There were two guy that she particularly enjoyed spending time with. One guy was Sebastian Parsons, son of a wealthy businessman. He wasn't much older than her. His father didn't have the time or inclination to dress up and go out so sent his son instead. The company, Mediglobe, which would soon be owned by Sebastian, had something to do with transporting medicine globally to deprived countries (or so Lucy gleaned from listening in to the conversations) and had won several awards. The prestigious, black tie award evenings required a 'plus one' from its guests. The company itself, hosted many charity auctions and fancy dinner parties where the rich and the richer were invited to donate money. Sebastian didn't have a girlfriend, nor did he want one. Work kept him busy and once girls found out how much money he had, their eyes sparkled and they clung on for longer than he appreciated.

Lucy on the other hand, was happy to accompany Sebastian when asked to, knowing that she would be wined and dined and leave richer than she had arrived. It was a bonus that he was good looking. He had a mop of curls – not dissimilar to hers and being the same age, they had lots to talk about.

The other guy that Lucy had enjoyed spending time with was Matteo Lorenzo, or Matt for short. He was Italian and insanely beautiful as men go, he was from wealthy parents before he'd inherited even more money from his grandmother who had been, as rumour had it, married into Italian Mafia, Lucy didn't know if there was an ounce truth in it, but she never felt in any danger at all when she was around him, quite the opposite really. He had dark skin and dark hair and his accent was a delight to listen to. Being born into money, he stank of it. Initially, she had thought him arrogant and self-obsessed, but soon realised that he didn't know any better, this was just how he had always lived his life. He made it his business to be invited to high class events, fashion shows, business dinners and anything else associated with likeminded people who lived in the stench of money. Lucy could really understand where the phrase 'filthy rich' came from as she smiled and clinked glasses with the faux-friendly. These people, no matter how rich, did not seem to live happy lives.

Lucy, nevertheless, enjoyed these events. She enjoyed being the envy of other women (usually older than her) who would smile at Matteo in hopes of a response. Matt was about 14 years older than her and the age gap would not be her personal choice, but this wasn't the usual sort of relationship, this was business. Besides, she wondered from time to time with things that he said, if he preferred the company of guys.

Things were going well. Lucy was earning more money than she cared to calculate. She'd paid off her credit card debt in a matter of weeks and enjoyed the best social life. If she'd discovered this line of work sooner, she would have been able to keep her horse – and on full livery, she mused. By her final term in university, with work load being at its highest, her work as an escort was slowing down. She had to turn down work and was now only escorting Sebastian three times a month and Matteo once. It suited her.

One Wednesday evening, the taxi dropped her off outside the theatre hall. She'd been on edge for some reason today and was constantly looking over her shoulder. Thankfully, Matt's was often heard before his hand appeared on her waist and she heard him thank the valet as he handed over the keys, "Don't scratch the paintwork," he joked.

"Ahh the Lovely Lucy!" he smiled at her and extended his hand in greeting. "You look ravishing as always." He kissed both cheeks and waited for her response.

"Why thankyou Matt," she eyed him up and down, because she knew he liked to think she fancied him, "You sure look good in blue, is it new?"

"Oh Lucy, I never wear things twice," he winked at her and held out his arm for her to link.

They walked through the double doors and up the grand staircase. Usually when Lucy was here, it was to enjoy a musical with her friends. Tonight, Matt was hosting a charity fashion show to raise money for famine torn third world countries.

"Come meet my girls," he suddenly took her down a corridor to the side of the main auditorium. There was hustle and bustle as the girls backstage were being dressed, made up, and having their outfits tweaked or sewn onto them. The girls all swooned over Matt as he thanked them all by name.

One girl in particular seemed to want to get Matt on his own, "Matteo," she whined from the seat where she was having her hair done. He held up his hand as if to tell her to wait her turn and Lucy noticed that she pouted and narrowed her eyes. Whereas the other girls all seemed to dispel the stereotypical attitudes of models with their smiling and obvious consumption of sugary sweets – there were bags of crisps and sweets littered all over, the pouty girl did not. She acted exactly how Lucy imagined models to act. Her scowling eyes followed Matt as he fussed around the younger and newest girls, demonstrating his strut, the pouty girl was clearly the one who had been there longer than all of them, and she clearly thought she should have the most attention.

Eventually, Matt took Lucy's arm and wandered over in her direction. "Maddison, you really should try to smile more." She stood up, and they kissed each other on each cheek. She did smile at him then.

Then she looked at Lucy, "Do you mind?"

Matt stopped Lucy from moving by putting his arm around her, "Lucy is my guest, be nice."

Lucy felt uncomfortable and she didn't like it. "It's okay Matt, I'll head back out and find our seats?"

"Nonsense, you are here with me. Maddison is just jealous," and then to Maddison directly, "You are quite rude sometimes. Remind me why I still pay you to work for me?"

Maddison stood up and whispered something in Matt's ear. Matt spoke with only his eyes. Maddison then turned around, picked up a hair brush and clenched in her fist, she stared into the mirror and her eyes followed Lucy with a scowl as they left. *No one crosses Maddison Pritchard, no one.* In one quick, movement, she snapped the wooden handle off the brush and threw it at the mirror, which cracked. The other girls in the room didn't even notice, they were used to her tantrums.

The fashion show was a great success and Lucy could see why Matt continued to pay Maddison to work his fashions shows, she was a stunner and really got the attention of the crowd.

At the end of the evening, Matt thanked Lucy for accompanying him and promised her that if she ever needed anything, she should come to him. He would sort everything – probably by throwing money at the situation. Lucy assured him, waving her now full purse in his direction, that he was already doing so.

"Seriously Lucy, anytime. You just ask."

Chapter 26

Another evening, when she was joining Sebastian for one of his charity auctions, she caught him looking at her from the bar. For some reason, the way he looked at her made her stomach jump. She had always been strict with herself, no paid extras, and to be fair, most of the early guys she had worked with had been married, gay, or older and just wanted company and someone to show off. But when she had met Sebastian, she had felt differently. Nothing had ever happened in the weeks that she had been escorting him, but she hadn't ever verbally made her terms *known* as she had with the others. She admittedly found him hot and if he happened to want more than this, Lucy would have a hard time saying no. As his gaze intensified, she was suddenly nervous. This was more than just appreciation of her company. She smiled, turned back to her drink and took a sip before taking herself off to the ladies to check her hair and take a moment's respite.

They were in the car when he asked her outright, "I would like you to spend the night with me Lucy."

Silence. Lucy had almost been expecting him to ask but still hadn't worked out what her response would be.

"I'm sorry," he sounded genuine, "That was rude of me to ask so forthrightly."

"I, um, I don't do," she paused, "I don't do extras." She looked at him; his eyes, his long eyelashes, his mouth, his jaw. *Shit.*

"It doesn't have to be work," he suggested.

Her heart pounded in her chest as she thought for a moment. She *was* attracted to him and of all the guys she had met in this job, he was the only one that she could see herself actually choosing for if they had met in a conventional way. She bit her lip and against her fighting against her moral compass – this was technically prostitution - she nodded. "I won't accept any money for it," she lifted her eyes to look at him and as she did, he took hold of her chin.

"You are the most beautiful woman I have ever met and I have wanted to do this for quite a while now." He kissed her and right in that moment, she didn't care about how she's met him, she didn't care about the money, she didn't care that this would be just one night. She wanted him more than she had ever wanted anyone in her life. The hairs on her arms stood on end and she felt a twist in her groin.

The driver dropped them off at his apartment in the centre of the city and she could see how different he was to Matt. Sebastian had money, but didn't stink of it. He lived a regular life. He lived a bachelor life and admittedly lived on microwave meals. But this evening there was no small talk as he led her straight to his bedroom.

He held her at arm's length and took in her beauty. She trembled, feeling his gaze move down over her body and knowing that he wanted her, a guy who could have his pick of any woman, wanted her, made her light headed. Feeling bold, she started to unbutton his shirt and then it was his turn to shudder.

Lucy hadn't had many physical relationships. She wasn't one for one night stands and didn't like to jump into bed with her boyfriends on the first date. She preferred to get to know them before she decided if she wanted to be intimate with them. In all fairness, most guys got annoyed at her reluctance and so, Sebastian would only be the third person she had ever been with intimately. She wasn't sure how she felt, but she was sure that she could change her mind and he would be okay with that. She 'knew him' – ish: she had escorted him to more dinner dates than she cared to recall, her bank balance was testament to that.

"Are you sure about this?" Sebastian whispered.

Instead of gracing him with an answer, finishing unbuttoning his shirt, she kissed his chest and then his stomach as she unbuttoned his trousers where his erection was obvious. Before she could go any further, his arms were lifting her back up to standing.

"My turn," he turned her around and started to pull down the zip of her dress. As he started to slide the satin dress from her shoulders, she heard his breath rasping as he took in her appearance. He unclasped her bra and turned her around. Every nerve in her body was on high alert and yet she felt so comfortable, so safe, so turned on.

He pulled her close and inhaled her scent. This was the first time he had been on a date more than once with a woman before getting half naked. And, he had never brought them back here. Usually, he took them to a hotel. Why Lucy was different? He didn't know, he just wanted to feel connected to her on a deeper level. He wanted to be inside her. It was the first time he had ever felt like this.

The next morning, Lucy sat up in bed and thought back on the night before. Sebastian came back from the kitchen and handed her a cup of tea. The sex had been, nice, which is possibly the worst adjective to describe something that should have been amazing. She'd wondered at one point if he had been nervous because he'd gone a bit quiet and sheepish. She'd even gotten the feeling that he wanted more than a one night stand but he hadn't said anything to confirm this so she was happy to let things run their course. Maybe a second time with him would be different. Or if not, then perhaps there was a reason he didn't have relationships and used an escort agency.

His phone rang, he looked at the number and left the room.

She'd sat looking out of the window when her phone beeped, checking for messages, she realised that it was running out of charge – she wouldn't have thought to take a charger out with her, she didn't usually stay out all night. She walked over to the desk at the far end of the dining room where Sebastian had set up a work space. Surely there would be charger somewhere on there. She started to move piles of papers and books carefully, to see if there was. Nope. Maybe he kept it in a drawer. She opened the top drawer, pens. Second, photographs of women and prices per night. Urgh. So there had been others before her, grim.

Unable to find a charging cable, she went to see if he had finished the call, as she got closer to the door, she could hear his side of the phone call.

"Are we on schedule?"

"How many girls this time?"

"All," he paused and then walked further away from the doorway and Lucy struggled to hear what he was saying, but she heard enough "Young?"

"14-18? Nice work."

"Wednesday's truck?"

"Great, thanks. I'll make sure the authorities have somewhere else to focus their attention. You'll have a clear run off the ship. Keep me updated. While we're on the phone, I just need to ask about -" His voice grew quieter as he walked further away from the door.

Lucy stood up and walked over to the window. Young girls? 14-18? On a truck? She took a moment to process this information and suddenly, connecting some dots, whether in the right order or not, she ran back over to the desk and opened the drawer. She rifled through the pictures. Realising quickly that these girls were not dressed as escorts, they were in clothes that did not fit, hair unkempt and the prices were 'selling prices.' Some of the girls looked far too young. She felt sick.

A few moments later, he sauntered back into the room. She was facing the window, not wanting him to see her face. She saw his reflection in the glass, he looked proud of himself. Lucy needed to get out. But before she did, she needed to work out what to do with what she'd just overheard; should she confront him? Could she have put two and two together and gotten five? She played it aloof with him. Not that he noticed, let alone seem bothered by it. When he went to the toilet, Lucy used the last bit of charge on her phone to take a quick photo of the contents of the drawer.

Just before lunch she smiled at Sebastian and asked, "Is there any chance you can get me a taxi? I have an assignment to finish before Monday." It was a complete lie, she was up to date with everything as usual.

"I can do one better," he walked over and put his arms around her waist. "I will take you home myself."

"Oh," she tried not to sound as uncomfortable as she felt. "That's great. I'll just grab my things." Her things consisted of her clutch and keys but the need for distance from him was greater now than it had ever been."

Once in the car, he handed her an envelope with her money, instinctively she took it and then seeing that there was more than usual she added, "I said I didn't want paying for last night."

He looked sideways at her and smiled, "You can class it as a gift from me then."

She put it in her clutch, forced a smile on her face, "Thank you." There was absolutely no way she was banking that money. All of a sudden, she felt so cheap she wanted to cry.

Back in her room, she turned on the shower. She needed to wash every bit of last night from her. She undressed and climbed into the shower, the too-hot water searing her skin. Once the tears had run dry, and she'd scrubbed her skin raw, she started to process everything she had seen and heard. If she had connected the dots correctly, Sebastian was bringing these 'young' women into the country on his medical trucks and making sure that the trucks weren't being searched by creating a fuss elsewhere. He was trafficking women on his father's charity medical trucks and probably making a fortune. Money that he had just paid her in cash.

Seconds later, she was leaning over the toilet, throwing up. Not only was she a cheap whore, she was profiting from the trafficking and prostitution of young girls. She wrapped herself in a towel and picked up the phone. The number for the local police was pinned as standard to the notice board in each dorm room and she did not hesitate to call them.

An hour later, two officers were at the reception waiting for her. They headed towards a table in the cafeteria. Lucy gave a brief overview of the phone call and showed them the few hurried and slightly blurred photographs that she had on her phone, thinking that would be enough. But they had more questions for her.

"How did you meet Sebastian?" the male officer asked her.

Shit. "I accompany him to charity events." Lucy looked at her cup of tea with sudden intent.

"Can you elaborate?" the female officer was writing in her notebook.

"I am accompany him to dinners and charity events so that he doesn't have to go alone."

"And are you paid for your time?"

"I don't have sex for money."

"That's not what I asked. I asked if you were paid for the evenings you spent with Sebastian."

Lucy hung her head, "Yes." She looked at the female officer, "I wanted to clear my credit card bill before I graduated."

The officer nodded. "So you don't have sex with your," she chose the next word carefully, "clients?"

Lucy cried. "Not usually," she covered her face and her shoulders trembled. "I've been working for him for ages and he liked me and asked me to stay over last night. It was the first time and I said I didn't want paid for it."

"You had sex with him last night?" The male officer clarified.

"And stayed over. That's where I was when I heard the phone call this morning. Please don't say I will get into trouble for this, I am about to graduate as a teacher and it would ruin my career before it has even started," she pleaded.

The officers looked at each other.

"We will look into this," the female officer closed her notebook and waved it at Lucy. "In the meantime, I don't think you need reminding that you should probably not spend any more time with Mr Parsons." Lucy nodded.

***

Sitting on the toilet seat in the ladies loos, Lucy had managed to calm her nerves, she had lost all the happy vibe from her hen party and she needed to get out of here without *him* seeing her. She had ruined Sebastian's life. The police had found his father's medical supplies truck coming off a ship at port and had searched it. They had found fourteen girls all underage, hiding in the back of the lorry. No doubt promised money to start a new life and undoubtedly lied to. The driver had been arrested and Sebastian's father had been picked up by officers shortly afterwards. Thanks to her statement, Sebastian had been picked up within minutes of the truck being searched. She'd hidden in her room for days following the whole newsworthy event and had only ventured out when she knew that Sebastian would be sent to prison for his crimes.

What she hadn't banked on, was her name being used in the statement. She had hoped she would have been able to remain anonymous. A couple of weeks afterwards, Sebastian's father had asked the police to arrange contact so that he could speak to her in person.

"I want to thank you for salvaging what was left of my company's reputation." he'd told her. "Putting an end to the underhand works of my son was very brave of you."

It was an awkward meeting during which, Lucy hadn't said much.

Needless to say, Sebastian was written out of the inheritance, the company name dragged through the press, it wouldn't have been worth much in the end.

After all the publicity and with her graduation looming, Lucy had change her name via deed poll. She graduated as Lucy Lawrence, her mother's maiden name and had laid the whole sorry situation to rest.

Sebastian was sentenced to nine years. It would appear that he had been released early seeing as he was sat out there, in the same bar as her and her friends. She mustered all her strength to unlock the toilet door and out of the ladies bathroom. Instead of heading back into the bar, she turned left and headed out towards the garden area at the rear. She would just call her friends and tell them she'd been ill and had to go home. She opened the door, walked through the garden to the gate at the back and was just about to unlatch it when she heard his voice.

"Didn't want to introduce me to your friends?"

She didn't turn around.

"Look at me, you bitch."

Taking a deep breath, she mustered all her courage and turned around to face him.

He stood closer to her. His breath made her wince, "You ruined my life."

"You ruined your own life," she was surprised at the venom in her own voice. "You ruined countless women's lives when you sold them into the sex slave."

"You didn't mind the money lining your pocket though, did you?"

"I didn't know what you were doing," she sounded defensive.

He pushed her up against the wall just outside the beer garden, which was stupidly empty today. "My parents killed themselves because of the shame you brought when you told the police." There was no remorse for his own actions. "You did that."

He slapped her around the face sending her off balance. He pulled her to her feet by her hair and then punched her in the stomach. Once again he pulled her to her feet. Pushing her face up against the wall, he smirked. "You're a tough one, aren't you?" She looked at him, unemotional and unfeeling. This last year had made her tough.

"Fuck you," she spat in his face.

"You don't learn, do you?" He was laughing now. "I can do whatever I want to you. Cute little school teacher – with a past to be ashamed of!" He pushed her face roughly into the wall and stepped back. She knew that he was about to kick her and with the little energy she had left, she moved slightly to avoid most of the force.

He grabbed her by her hair again and dug his fingers into the soft spot of her skull, the point where her skull had caved in during the first attack. "You heal fast, don't you?" He was breathing into her ear now. "You should have died that night. A life for a life. But you didn't." He threw her to the ground, "I promise you, you will. One day, when you are not expecting it. I will kill you and your boyfriend. You will pay for ruining my life Lucy Lawrence."

He left her lying in the alleyway at the back of the beer garden. She watched him walk away. She was shaking as she reached for her phone.

"Penny? Help me. Beer garden," was all she could muster and less than a minute later, she was surrounded by her friends and staff from the bar.

After she had cleaned herself up at Penny's house, Lucy asked Penny to call Alex. And whilst she did, Lucy called a number that she had kept in her phone for the last seven years.

"Matteo?"

His silky Italian accent sang down the phone to her, "Yes, speaking?" his voice sang in his beautiful accent down the phone.

"My name is Lucy, Lucy Lawrence. About seven years ago, I -"

He cut her off, "You do not need to explain who you are Lucy, I remember you well my friend. But why are you calling me now?"

"You promised that if I ever needed anything, I was to call you," Lucy held her breath.

"Ah, my preeetty Lucy. You need me now?"

She burst into tears.

"Lucy where are you? I will come right away. Tell me where you are."

Chapter 27

Alex had arrived at Penny's house first, devastated to see Lucy traumatised and beaten, again. It made no sense, the man was behind bars. How on earth was this possible? He kept talking to himself,

"How the -?"

"But?"

"Why?"

Lucy was resting on Penny's sofa and Alex was pacing the living room when someone knocked on the front door. Penny answered it and then the strong recognisable Italian voice came echoing through from the hall and the open front door, "I am here to see Lucy Lawrence."

When Matteo saw her beaten and bruised, he rushed to her, "My Lucy, my darling girl, who did this to you?" He sat down and put his arms around her to cradle her in such a way that Alex winced and sat down, even more confused than before.

Lucy didn't have time to explain, Sebastian was a man on the edge. By her reckoning, it was him who had beaten her nearly to death with a golf club. She almost certainly *would* be dead if Alex hadn't driven over to find her.

She looked at Alex, "I have nothing to hide and you can hear everything I need to say to Matt. I promise to tell you every sordid detail afterwards." She met his eyes and pleaded, "Don't hate me."

She turned to Matteo, "When I worked for you, I also met and worked with another man. Sebastian Parsons." Matteo was nodding.

"I have heard that name."

"His father owned Mediglobe, before he killed himself."

"Ah yes, now I recall," Matteo was shaking his head. "The son was buying and selling women?"

"Yes, using his father's company and name as a shield to hide behind. Until -" She covered her face with her hands and wept. Both Alex and Matt stood to comfort her, but Matt being closer was there quicker and Alex sat down, despondent.

Wiping her eyes, Lucy continued. "I stayed at Sebastian's flat one time," she didn't look up to see either of their expressions, "I wasn't paid to, I wanted to," she explained, trying to make it clear to them that she was not a whore.

"Oh Lucy, a lovely girl like you should not feel bad about sleeping with a rich man," he winked at her, "I am too old?" he laughed, trying to make her smile, "And, I am gay." He put his arm around her and shushed her again as he half laughed, half cried at his attempts to cheer her up.

"I found photographs of the girls and overheard him on the phone the next morning, arranging to bring girls into the country on the Mediglobe lorry. And I told the police." She was pale now, and shaking. "Sebastian was arrested and sentenced to prison but then his father killed himself and he was released early and he tried to kill me once already, but we didn't realise it was him…" Matt put his finger on her lips to quiet her as she tried to retell the whole of the last year in one sentence.

"What do you need from me?"

"I need to feel safe," she lifted her eyes and he nodded.

"I will sort it Lucy." He beckoned to Alex, "I think you need to tell your boyfriend about your past employment, yes?"

Lucy nodded.

Matteo left the living room and into the garden where they heard him talking on his phone in Italian. Alex, shoulders slouched, looked at Lucy. She beckoned him to sit down next to her. He didn't hesitate.

"What did you do, Lucy? What job?" He leaned into her his eyes pleading to be let out of his misery. "I am thinking the absolute worst here."

She took a deep breath, "I was an escort for the last year of university. No paid extras. Mostly older guys like Matt, all rich, all paid me for my company. That's all."

"And this other guy? He did this to you today?"

She nodded.

"And you slept with him?"

"Once. A long time ago."

"But he didn't pay you."

"I didn't want paying. I liked him."

Alex was quiet for a moment while he processed everything she had told him.

"And who is this Matteo?"

As if on demand, Matt walked back into the cubicle. "I am a fashionista, millionaire and my gr-" he paused, re-thought and then continued, "My family has links with people who can help. I do not agree with violence, until someone threatens the people I care about." He nodded towards Lucy. "My people are on their way to meet me now." He looked at his watch, "Two hours and I will hand it over to them and you will be safe." He sat on the chair that had been occupied by Alex,

"My people will find this monster and you will not hear from him again." He sat down and smiled at them. "Now

Lucy, this man seems to mean a lot to you. Is it love?" His eyes twinkled.

Lucy half smiled, "Today was my hen party."

"Oooh! A wedding! I will get an invite I hope?" he winked.

Alex stood. Lucy held her breath, "You will," Alex held out his hand. "You are going out of your way to protect the only girl I love. You are most definitely invited." They shook hands.

Matteo sat in the chair, made a few more calls and then stood, "You will stay in my hotel for now. I will get you anything you need until this is all over, yes?"

They both nodded, swept away in the speed of it all. They sat in the back of the Evoke and relaxed behind the tinted windows. Alex wondering when Lucy's nightmare would end and Lucy wondering if she would ever be free from the terror she had brought upon herself all those years ago. They were in the car for about forty minutes before Matteo pulled the Range Rover into a bay in front of the biggest hotel in the city. Lucy stepped out of the car and followed him in through the glass doors. She had been here before, many years ago when she was first escorting Matteo to dinner parties that he hosted here. Thinking back to those days made her feel uneasy.

Everything that had happened to her in the last year had been because of her choices back then. Bad choices? Good choices? Hell, she didn't have the brain capacity to think it through. In the penthouse a few minutes later, Matteo was giving keys and his contact number to Alex, Lucy was lying down on the sofa, she kicked off her shoes and pulled the cushions closer to support her aching body.

She got out her phone to text: *Hey Penny, Just arrived at Matts. Lying low for now. I'll call soon.*

There was an instant reply: *Love you girl, take care of yourself. You need anything doing here, just ask. Pen x*

No, we're all good. Alex staying too and not telling mum just yet. She'll just worry. Going to nap now.

Lucy put her phone on silent, pulled the throw from the back of the sofa over her and winced as she rolled onto her side. She'd survived a couple of broken ribs before, she could do it again. Especially, she thought, if Matteo was going to sort this problem out for her once and for all.

It was late when she woke up. Alex was watching a film sat at her feet and he moved to help her sit, she gasped in pain as she momentarily forgetting that she had broken ribs. "I need to get into bed. I need to lie flat, not curled up. Can you help me?"

He carefully lifted her in his arms and carried her to the bedroom where he laid her down on the bed. Penny had cleaned Lucy's bloodied skin as best she could, but her hair was still matted and there were blood stains around her hairline and under her chin. "Are you sure you wouldn't like a bath?" Alex suggested.

The prospect of a hot bath suddenly appealed and she agreed. While the bath was running, he helped her to undress. Tears pricked his eyes as he lifted her top and saw her bruised and battered body. She was so frail and fragile and bad things kept happening. He hoped that Matteo's men were able to put a stop to the bastard who did this. He wanted him dead more than anything and if he had to do it himself, he would give it his best shot.

Lucy lowered herself into the water. Her muscles stopped screaming in pain and relaxed. Alex knelt at the side of the bath and helped to wash her hair and clean the blood and mud from her face. He was gentle and even then, it hurt. Everything hurt. Her heart hurt too. "I am so sorry that I caused all of this," she wept.

"Lucy, you weren't to know."

"I am so ashamed of what I used to do."

"Lucy, darling. It's the things we do in our lives that shape us into the people we are. You wouldn't be the Lucy that I know and love if you hadn't experienced everything you have."

She sank deeper into the water, washing away all the dirt and filth of her past. She wouldn't choose the same things now, yet at the time, she hadn't seen anything wrong with it. Once she was washed, Alex helped her out of the bath and into one of the dressing gowns. She lay on the bed, rosy cheeks and wet hair. "Do you still love me?"

"More than you will ever know." He crawled carefully onto the bed beside her and together, they fell asleep.

Chapter 28

Lucy awoke the next morning to the sound of talking. Alex and - who was that other voice? She knew it, but couldn't place it. She rolled over, ouch. That hurt. She opened her eyes. Where was she? Sleepiness confused her for a few moments until she remembered that she wasn't at home and that the second voice she could hear was Matteo's. The strong painkillers she'd taken must have worked, as she'd had an undisturbed night. It was only now that the memories of the previous evening came flooding back as did the pain when she tried to sit up.

She wondered what they were talking about. Thinking about Sebastian made her heart race and she had to focus and calm herself down again.

Carefully, she shimmied to the edge of the bed and stood up. Wrapping her dressing gown as tight as she could, aware of her nakedness underneath, she wandered through the penthouse until she found both men in the small kitchen area.

"You are awake Lucy, my dear friend," Matt's Italian accent was as beautiful as ever.

"Barely," she croaked, "I need coffee."

Alex was on the case instantly.

Lucy perched on the stool and inhaled the hot coffee, frothy coffee, hmmm. The caffeine was already lifting her spirits when Matt spoke, "Your friend, Mr Parsons, will not be bothering you again."

Even Alex gasped at this. Matteo had waited until Lucy was awake before bringing up the conversation.

"You didn't…." Lucy wanted to ask if he was dead, but changed her mind. *Don't ask questions you don't want the answer to* was a motto that they lived by at school.

"Lucy, I am not a murderer." The indignant look on Matteo's face was a picture. "Although, right about now, he will wish I was." Laughter filled the space around them. Lucy wanted to know, Alex wanted to know but Matteo was not letting on. "Let's put it this way. He is about to find out what it like to be sold into a trade he is not used to – manual labour in a third world country is hard. The heat, the lack of shade, lack of water…" He shook with mirth and looked at his watch, "He's about to do a full day's work for the first time in his life."

"Will he come back?"

"Not without his passport."

"He doesn't have it?"

Matteo took a passport from his pocket. "No he does not," then he added, "And passport control will have a hard

265

time allowing him back into England with the penalties and sanctions they have on record for him.

Lucy looked confused, "How?"

"Lucy, Lucy, have you yet to realise what money can buy?" he cocked his head to the right and looked at her. "It buys many things, for many people. Team that with my family connections and you get a lot of power, very quickly. He won't ever bother you again. You have my word."

"Thanks Matt," she smiled weakly. "You've done so much for me, after so many years."

"Lucy, I liked you from the first night you joined me. I could tell that you were one of the nicest people I would ever meet. I knew you were struggling with debt and working to pay it off and I hired you as my escort because I knew that you would not accept money from me if I simply tried to help you. You like to feel that you are earning your money, no?"

She blushed and nodded.

"I have far too much money, it sickens me and yet, I cannot spend it fast enough. I have everything I have ever wanted," he flicked his hands around the penthouse, "Except for love. Money cannot buy that. Money attracts greed most of the time and those people are not nice. You are not like those people. You, Lucy, have a heart of gold and work to please others, not for praise of self-gratification."

Alex tried to speak, failed and put his arm around Lucy. He was proud of her as well.

"You two love birds have a wedding to plan, yes?" Matteo nodded at them. "You should do that."

Lucy, cheered up instantly, forgot the aches and pains, stood up and threw her arms around Matteo. "Thank you, a million times," she beamed at him.

***

"Get your hands off me," Sebastian's voice cut through the hot, arid air.

The reply wasn't hard to work out, even if the words weren't in English. A machete in digging in your back would often get a response. He had been approached by two men in suits at about 8 p.m. yesterday and, in broad daylight, stuffed into the back seat of a tinted windowed 4 x 4. A huge hulk of a guy on either side had stopped him from breathing, let alone escaping. Hours and hours on a rickety propeller plane saw him here now. In the land of heat and sand. Very little to be seen anywhere and, a machete pointed at him if he didn't do as he was instructed. He needed water.

"Water?" he asked, miming drinking a glass of water.

One of the tall, skinny guys, face protected from the sun by a scarf and glasses, nodded to a bucket. Sebastian had thanked the guy and walked over, ready to scoop a handful of water from the bucket until he saw the colour of it. Brown

267

water. No thanks. He'd kicked the bucket over and earned himself another reminder of how sharp the machete was.

Another 10 minutes of walking and he was stood with seven other men. It was like a scene from Holes. Dessert, spade and digging. He growled under his breath. "Lucy Lawrence," he clenched his jaw and his fists automatically followed suit, that bitch of a woman would pay for what she had done to him.

***

Alex and Lucy's wedding day dawned, clear skies and brilliant sunshine. The leaves were rusting over and the ground was spattered with those that had already fallen. Maggie was helping Lucy into her dress and the hairdresser was ready with the veil, the photographer ready to capture the moment. Bursting with pride, Maggie dabbed her eyes with the corner of her handkerchief.

"You look beautiful Lucy," she smiled.

"I'm giddy," Lucy giggled, taking a sip of her drink.

"So you should be," Maggie kissed her.

The photographer took pictures from every angle. The bridesmaids, bride and mother, bride and bridesmaids playing the fool. It was the start of the most perfect day of her life.

Alex too was excited. Excited to make Lucy his wife and to finally move onto the next chapter of his life. Carl and Chris had arrived last night and they had shared beers, played cards and reminded each other of the stupid things they had done growing up. Alex didn't mind admitting that he was a bit nervous about what might be mentioned in the best man's speech.

The day couldn't have been more perfect and as day turned to evening, Lucy and Alex danced on the dance floor to a Celine Dion track, she leaned into him rested her head against his chest. She smiled. How much she loved this man. All the heartache and pain she'd endured on her journey to this day felt irrelevant now. She lifted her head and tiptoed to whisper in his ear, "I guess, now that we're married, I can tell you without shame that I'm pregnant?"

His eyes almost popped out of their sockets, "What? When did you find that out?"

"I suspected yesterday, but didn't do a test until this morning."

He was still grinning as he kissed her and then picked her up in his arms and spun her around. She shrieked in delight.

"So," he placed her gently down on the floor and pulled her closer, "So, this is love." They kissed and danced until their feet were sore, their cheeks aching from smiling and their eyelids ready for closing. Life was pretty perfect.

***

Blue flashing lights lit up the evening sky. A man with his dog was huddled in the shadows talking to a police officer.

"My dog just ran into the garden and started barking, wouldn't come out when I called. I went in after him and that's when I saw her. Sitting in her chair. I thought she was asleep at first. Then a car went passed and the headlights shone in and I knew she was dead."

That was when he'd called 999.

Paramedics were bringing out a woman, late thirties, early forties on a stretcher, in a zipped up bag. Forensic police were taking photographs inside the house and were talking into radios, no sign of forced entry and no apparent foul play.

The neighbours came out to speak to the police. This was the lady who hadn't left the house in over a year. Not since her son had been killed in a road accident. She had accepted very little help when her husband had been held on a custodial sentence. She didn't answer the door, the phone, sometimes food parcels were accepted and at other times, left to rot on the doorstep. Although they saw her curtains twitch every now and again, she refused any offered help and eventually the neighbours had moved on with their own lives.

Megan Simpson had died, broken-hearted at the loss of her only son and the imprisonment of her husband. She simply sat down one day and never got back up. The two people that had filled her life with happiness had both been taken from her so quickly. Her heart had broken in two.

When they found her, in the armchair, she was holding in her hand a photograph of the three of them the day Thomas had been born. Michael and her, smiles so wide and a new-born baby, asleep in her arms.

"Died of a broken heart," one police officer was telling another.

"Love does that to you."

"Poor woman."

A young paramedic looked at the outline of the woman's body through the bag. She took a breath, "So this -" she waved her hands around in the air, "- is love?" She shook her head. "No thanks."

With that she followed the stretcher into the back of the ambulance.

Special Thanks

There are so many people who have helped me with this novel and I would like to take the time to thank each of them for giving up there time in already packed schedules. I am so grateful.

Karen GJ, I loved your enthusiasm for a book that was nothing like your usual genre. You read it, told me truthfully that my ending was rubbish and gave me wonderful ideas of where the story could twist and turn to. I feel like I have written two novels that came together beautifully. I cannot thank you enough for helping me to write my best work to date.

Natalie, your experience in the first aid field was invaluable. Who knew I knew so little! You were always on hand, day and night when I had questions or when I sent you extracts to check. Thank you for your friendship and support throughout this project.

Yvonne, my beautiful friend, therapist and coincidentally, ex-cop, thank you. The hours that we spent checking all the facts over lattes. You are an amazing woman and you knowledge of the inner workings of police procedure helped me to make this book real. I cannot thank you enough for helping me to fix the MANY mistakes! Oh how naïve I am!

My friend and colleague, Pauline, the cover artwork is amazing. I cannot believe how our first ideas could turn into an actual oil pastel piece of art. It is framed and on my wall. The book would not be the same without it. Thank you.

Then to the people who read, reviewed, found mistakes, gave me tips on layout and size and font and all the things that I never would have considered. Watching and checking all my social media posts and basically filling me with confidence: Lynn, Hollie, Amy, Samantha, Megan, Kelly, Sue, Gill – you guys are amazing, Thank

About the Author

Maddie Richardson is a Lancashire based author who penned her first thriller in 2022.

She worked with horses for the first part of her adult life before deciding at 25 years old it was time to think about the 'grown up stuff.' She completed a part time degree with the Open University whilst working to pay her rent and after seven years of studying, she qualified as a teacher.

Maddie lives a contented life in a rural Lancashire village with her husband and son.

She is planning her next novel.

Printed in Great Britain
by Amazon

81436437R00161